"I'm not the man for you, Tave."

She straightened to her full height. "Don't I get to decide that on my own?"

Daniel shook his head. "No. I'm going to decide it for you. I'm a drifter with no money or family. I want you to understand I have nothing to give you."

She stared at him. "Can you give me love?"

His eyes grew wide. "Wh–what?"

She squared her shoulders and clenched her fists at her sides. "Savannah told me she could tell that you're in love with me. As embarrassing as it is for me to ask, I have to know. Do you love me?"

He hesitated for a moment, and she held her breath. His shoulders drooped as if his whole body had deflated. "Yes, I love you. More than I ever thought it possible to love someone else."

Her heart pounded, and she frowned. "Then what's the problem? I've fought my feelings for you, but I can't anymore." She stepped closer. "I love you, too, Daniel."

He held up his hands as if to warn her to stay back. "No, I won't saddle you with a man who can't give you everything that Matthew can."

"Matthew? What does he have to do with this? I don't love him. I love you."

He reached out and grabbed her by the shoulders. "It doesn't matter. I won't keep you from the life you deserve." He released her with such force that she stumbled back. "I have to leave."

Icy fear gripped her. "Leave?"

"Yes. When I'm gone, you'll know I was right."

SANDRA ROBBINS and her husband live in the small college town where she grew up. Until a few years ago she was working as an elementary school principal, but God opened the door for her to become a full-time writer. Without the help of her wonderful husband, four children, and five grandchildren who have supported her dreams for many years, it would be impossible to write. As a child, Sandra accepted Jesus as her Savior and has depended on Him to guide her throughout her life. It is her prayer that God will use her words to plant seeds of hope in the lives of her readers. To find out more about Sandra and her books, go to her Web site at http://sandrarobbins.net.

Books by Sandra Robbins

HEARTSONG PRESENTS
HP919—The Columns of Cottonwood

Dinner at the St. James

Sandra Robbins

Heartsong Presents

To Vera, Martha, and Nancy for your service in our church library. You are a blessing to our members.

A note from the Author:
I love to hear from my readers! You may correspond with me by writing:

Sandra Robbins
Author Relations
PO Box 721
Uhrichsville, OH 44683

ISBN 978-1-61626-222-8

DINNER AT THE ST. JAMES

All scripture quotations are taken from the King James Version of the Bible.

All of the characters and events in this book are fictitious. Any resemblance to actual persons, living or dead, or to actual events is purely coincidental.

Our mission is to publish and distribute inspirational products offering exceptional value and biblical encouragement to the masses.

PRINTED IN THE U.S.A.

one

May 1878
Outside Willow Bend, Alabama

Tave Spencer, the teacher in the one-room schoolhouse in Willow Bend, Alabama, sank into the chair behind her desk and blew at a strand of hair that dangled over her forehead. Just minutes before, she'd seen her well-behaved, attentive students transformed into a stampeding herd, each one bent on being the first to escape the classroom and begin the school-free days of summer. They'd dashed out the door without a backward glance at the teacher who'd hammered reading, math, and spelling into their heads for the past nine months.

She glanced around the almost-empty classroom and smiled at the one student who still remained. Gabby Rinaldi, the six-year-old daughter of Dante and Savannah Rinaldi, sat at her desk on the front row, her attention directed to the book she held.

"Gabby, your mother said she was going to pick you up today. I'm sure she'll be here any time now."

The child glanced up, and a smile curled her lips. She tilted her head to one side, her dark eyes sparkling behind the long lashes so much like her mother's. "She wanted to go into town to see the *Montgomery Belle*. Poppa says he can't keep Mama away from the docks when Captain Hawkins's boat pulls up to the landing. I guess she's watching them unload."

Tave chuckled. Everyone in the community knew that when

one of the steamboats docked at Willow Bend, Savannah Rinaldi would be somewhere nearby. Picking up her child at school gave her the perfect excuse to stop by the dock.

Tave picked up the books she planned to take home for the summer and nodded. "I'm sure you're right. Why don't we sit outside and wait for her?"

Together they walked from the schoolhouse, and Tave locked the door behind her. A twinge of sadness gripped her heart as she sat down beside Gabby on the front steps. She thought of the boys and girls she'd taught this past year and the progress they'd made.

She'd come to love every one of them and hated to see the school year draw to a close. Some of them, such as Tad Thompson and Johnny Williams, wouldn't return in the fall. They'd be needed on the farms, and their education would come to a halt.

Others, such as Gabby Rinaldi, were just starting their formal schooling and would be back. Tave smiled at Gabby. "When you come back to school in the fall, your brother will get to come with you."

Gabby nodded, and her dark curls bobbed up and down. "He can already read. Me and Poppa. . ." Her eyes grew wide, and she spread her short fingers over her mouth to stifle a gasp. "I mean Poppa and I have been teaching him."

Tave laughed and slipped her arm around the child's shoulders. "What a good sister you are. And a good student, too."

Gabby smiled up at her and then directed her gaze down the road that led to Willow Bend. Tave leaned back on the steps, closed her eyes, and lifted her face up to the late May sunshine.

Soon it would be hot along the Alabama River that twisted and turned through the Black Belt of Alabama, so called because of its rich, black soil that covered the area. Tave dreaded the hot days that were before them and the mosquitoes that bred in the vegetation along the edge of the river. After the mild winter they'd had, she suspected the annoying insects would emerge in high numbers.

Tave blinked her eyes open as Gabby jumped to her feet. "Mama's coming."

Shading her eyes with her hand, Tave stared in the direction Gabby pointed. Savannah's buggy came into sight, and Gabby hopped to the bottom of the steps to await her mother. When Savannah pulled the horse to a stop beside them, she flashed an apologetic smile in Tave's direction.

"I'm sorry. I ran into Martha Thompson in Mr. Perkins's store, and I couldn't get away." She reached out to pull Gabby into the buggy. Drawing the child close, Savannah planted a kiss on her forehead. "And how was your last day at school?"

"At least I didn't have to walk home today." Gabby snuggled next to her mother. "I don't want to stay home for the summer. I want to come back to school."

Tave laughed. "I wish all my students felt that way. But don't worry, you'll have such a good time at Cottonwood this summer, you'll hardly think of school."

Savannah nodded. "And Vance will get to come with you next fall." She glanced at Tave. "Why don't you let me drive you home? We can visit on the way."

"Are you going my way?"

"Yes. The *Montgomery Belle* still hadn't arrived when I left town. I thought I'd go back and see if it's there yet." Savannah let her gaze drift over the school grounds. "I'll never understand why the town didn't build this school right in the middle of Willow Bend. You have quite a walk coming out here every day."

Tave shook her head and climbed in the buggy. "It's less than a mile, and I like being so close to the river here. We get to see all the steamboats as they pass by."

Savannah turned the horse around and headed back to the small settlement. "I've always liked to watch them, too. I thought the *Montgomery Belle* would dock before I left Mr. Perkins's store, but it still wasn't there."

Gabby glanced up at Tave and grinned. "We thought you might be watching them unload, Mama."

Savannah shook her head. "No, I don't have time for that today. As soon as we let Miss Spencer out and I see the *Montgomery Belle*, we need to hurry home. Mamie is watching Vance, and that boy can be a handful."

Tave scooted back into the leather seat of the buggy. "Thanks for the ride. This last day of school has worn me out. I'm going to fix Poppa and me some supper. Then I think I'll go to bed early."

Savannah flicked the reins across the horse's back. "Are you going to help your father in his practice this summer?"

"Yes. I don't know how he makes it without someone to help run his office, but he refuses to hire anybody. I help out every chance I get, but I have to admit medicine has never appealed to me. I can't stand the sight of blood."

Savannah smiled. "Well, your father is the best doctor I've ever known. We're lucky to have him in Willow Bend."

"I think he's pretty wonderful, too."

Savannah tightened her hands on the reins and cast a sly glance in Tave's direction. "Is there anyone else around here that you think is wonderful besides your father?"

The question puzzled Tave. Her eyes grew wide, and she sat up straight. "No, not that I can think of."

"Not even Matthew Chandler?"

Now she understood. Tave's face warmed, and her breath caught in her throat at the mention of the heir to Winterville Plantation. "What makes you ask about Matthew?"

Savannah took her gaze off the road long enough to cast a knowing grin in Tave's direction. "Don't act so shocked. Everybody in Willow Bend knows he's been calling on you for the past year. That seems like a long time if you're not interested in him. In a romantic way, I mean. But after the way he teased you when you and your father first moved here, I didn't think you'd ever like him."

"I don't know if I've forgiven him or not." Tave turned in the seat toward Savannah. "Do you remember how he made fun of my name?"

Savannah laughed and nodded. "He did until you punched him in the nose at church one day and told him you were named after your grandmother Octavia and that your mother had shortened it to Tave. Then you held your fist in front of his face and dared him to make fun of your name again. Your father was mortified."

Tave cast a glance at Gabby to see if she'd overheard, but her student appeared to be asleep. "I was just a child then, but he left me alone after that." She sighed. "And now he shows up at our house quite often."

Tave wrinkled her forehead in thought about Matthew. It was true Matthew had visited with her and her father many times during the past year. At times she thought he came to argue with her father over their differing opinions concerning the war that had ended thirteen years ago but still produced some of the most heated discussions in west-central Alabama.

An image of Matthew's face flashed across her mind. Was she interested in him romantically? With his dark hair and flashing eyes, he was undoubtedly the best-looking bachelor in the county. And every single young woman she knew prayed to be the recipient of his attention. The fact that he'd picked her from all the available young women thrilled her and yet left her puzzled. After all, she was the daughter of a country doctor, and Matthew helped his father run one of the largest plantations in all of Alabama. The number of tenant farmers they supported was twice what the Rinaldis had at Cottonwood.

Savannah arched an eyebrow and stared at Tave. "Well, are you going to answer me?"

"I—I don't know what to say. Matthew is a friend. He hasn't mentioned anything more than that." Tave sighed. "I suppose I should be flattered that he likes me. After all, I'm not getting any younger, and there aren't that many young men my age in Willow Bend."

Savannah reached out to Gabby, who'd drifted off to sleep, and turned her so that her head rested in Savannah's lap. "Yeah. Twenty years is really old. That was my age when Dante and I married."

Tave always felt a little envious when she thought of Savannah and Dante's marriage. She'd often wondered if she would ever experience such great love in her life. She sighed and brushed at some dirt that had billowed up from the road and settled on her skirt. "You've told me your and Dante's romantic love story. Sometimes I think that's what I want: a handsome young man to sweep me off my feet. My practical side, however, tells me that's never going to happen. I'll probably spend the rest of my life taking care of my father and end up an old maid who wants to talk about how life is changing in the South."

A low-pitched rumble drifted from the direction of town, and Savannah smiled. "There's the *Montgomery Belle*. Maybe I'll get to see Captain Hawkins before I go back to Cottonwood."

The buildings that made up the small settlement of Willow Bend came into view, and Tave strained to catch a glimpse of the towering smokestacks of the big steamboat that plied the Alabama River. As their buggy trotted past the livery stable and the feed and grain store on the right, Tave wondered why no one was in sight today.

As they approached the general store, Tave sat up straight and frowned. Mr. Perkins, the elderly owner, shuffled out the front door of the store and followed several men who ran across the street toward the riverbank where a crowd had gathered. Their attention appeared riveted on the steamboat that sat moored to the dock at the foot of the bank.

"Something's happened," Tave murmured.

Frowning, Savannah pulled the buggy to a stop. She touched Gabby's shoulder, and the child's eyes blinked open. "Stay in the buggy until I get back. I'm going to the *Montgomery Belle*."

Gabby nodded and closed her eyes.

Tave jumped from the buggy and hurried toward the crowd. She glanced over her shoulder and saw Savannah tie the horse's reins to the hitching post in front of the store before she followed.

Martha Thompson stood in the middle of the group who peered at the boat, and Tave eased up next to her. If anyone knew what was happening, it would be Martha. She had the reputation of knowing everything that occurred in their community.

"What happened, Martha?"

The wrinkles in the woman's face deepened. The bonnet that covered Martha's gray curls wobbled as she shook her head and frowned. "They say it's bad, Tave. Doc's on board right now."

Tave's eyes widened. Her father was on board the boat? "Is someone hurt?"

Martha shifted the basket she held in one hand to the other and nodded. "Dead most likely. Captain Hawkins caught some fellows in a card game on board, and you know he don't allow no gambling on his boat. When he tried to break up the group, one of them gamblers pulled a gun. A young man who works on the boat tried to wrestle the gun out of the man's hand, and he ended up gettin' shot for tryin' to help the captain."

"That's terrible." Tave's worried gaze scanned the big boat from its bow to the stern-mounted paddle wheel at the back, but her father was nowhere to be seen.

Beside her, Martha inched closer. "And that ain't all. They say that, in all the commotion after the shooting, that gambler ran out of the cabin. Some of the deckhands seen him jump overboard."

Tave had no idea who *they* were, but she felt sure Martha had all the facts right. "Do they know what happened to him?"

Martha shook her head. "Last they seen of him, he was swimmin' to the far side of the river. They don't know if he made it though." She shrugged. "So he either drowned or escaped. They don't know which."

Tave looked back at the boat, but her father still had not appeared. "And you think the man he shot is dead?"

Martha arched her eyebrows and directed a solemn stare in Tave's direction. "Now you know I ain't one to start rumors, but I heard one of the passengers who got off say he doubted if the young man could still be alive."

Savannah arrived in time to hear Martha's words. Her eyes grew wide, and she grasped Tave's arm. "Have you seen your father yet?"

Tave shook her head. "No, I don't know what part of the boat he's on." Her gaze drifted over the sleek vessel that bobbed in the water, its gangway already lowered and resting on the bank.

Movement caught her attention, and her father stepped through a doorway onto the lower deck from what she assumed was one of the cabins. He backed up against the railing and stopped as if waiting for someone to exit.

A man, supporting the weight of a man's legs, appeared in the doorway, and he eased onto the deck. Captain Hawkins and another man, who Tave assumed was a deckhand, emerged supporting the injured man's upper body.

They stopped in front of her father, and he bent down to say something then straightened. He pointed up the hill toward the small building that housed his office, strode to the lowered gangway, and headed in the direction he'd pointed. He stopped halfway up the hill to survey the slow procession that followed and then resumed his journey.

When he reached the gathered crowd at the top of the bluff, Tave stepped forward. "Poppa, do you need me to help you?"

Relief flickered in his eyes. "I'm glad you're here. I'm going to have to remove a bullet from this young man, and I need your help. Are you up to it?"

Even after all the years of helping her father, Tave's stomach churned at the thought of assisting in surgery, but it didn't matter. If her father needed her assistance, she would help in any way she could. Before she could speak, the men carrying the injured sailor passed by her, and she glanced at the face of the young man.

She'd never seen anyone so pale before. He must have lost a lot of blood. His wheat-colored hair tumbled over his forehead, and a grimace of pain covered his face. His eyes appeared to be clenched shut, and his teeth bit into his lower lip. A low moan rumbled in his throat.

Tave nodded to her father. "I'll be right there." Turning to Savannah, she clasped her friend's hand. "I have to go. Thanks for the ride."

A worried expression crossed Savannah's face. "I'll be praying that your father can save this young man."

Tave turned and ran past the men carrying the injured sailor as she hurried toward her father's office, her mind in a whirl of what awaited her. She dashed through the front door and was rolling up her sleeves when the men arrived carrying the patient.

Her father took command of the situation right away. He pointed to the other room. "Take him in there and put him on that table."

Tave reached for the apron that hung on a hook by the wall, tied it around her waist, and ran to stoke the fire in the stove. Lots of hot water would be needed in the next few hours. She had just set the big pot on the stove's eye when her father called out.

"Tave, I need you."

Captain Hawkins and the other two men stood opposite her father beside the surgery table when she walked into the room. She stopped beside her father, who had his fingers clamped on the patient's wrist and his gaze directed to the pocket watch he held. When he finished, he glanced at her. "Pulse 114. I don't like that."

Captain Hawkins stared at them. Sorrow lined his face, and his chin quivered. "Dr. Spencer, this boy's name is Daniel Luckett. He saved my life. Take care of him, and I'll pay you whatever it costs."

Tave's father nodded. "We'll do what we can, but there's no

telling what kind of internal damage has been done. And he's lost a lot of blood. How long are you going to be in Willow Bend?"

"We'll be leaving for our upriver trip to Montgomery within the hour, but I'll check on him when we come back downriver." Captain Hawkins placed his hand on the injured man's shoulder and squeezed. "Tell him for me that I'm sorry the man who shot him escaped. I'll tell the sheriff when we dock at Selma, and I'll pass the word along to the other ship captains to keep a lookout for him. But I doubt if that gambler will ever show his face on the Alabama River again."

Captain Hawkins and his men turned and left the room, her father following. He called over his shoulder. "I'll be ready to operate on Mr. Luckett in a few minutes, Tave. I'll be right back to get him ready. In the meantime, it might make him feel better if you'd bathe his face with some cool cloths."

Tave hurried to the pitcher on a table against the wall and grabbed a clean cloth from the drawer underneath. Holding the cloth over the washbowl, she poured water over the cloth and wrung it out.

When she stepped back beside the injured man, she glanced down at Daniel Luckett again. Even with the evidence of pain, she realized he had a handsome face. He was young, perhaps about her age, maybe a few years older. She wondered what had made him take a job on a steamboat. Perhaps if he lived, he would tell her.

She touched his forehead with the wet cloth and began to move it gently across his skin. Her fingers moved to his cheeks and across his mouth that puckered with pain. She rewet the cloth and wiped at his mouth and across the lower part of his face. A groan rolled from his throat, and his head twitched.

Without warning, his eyes blinked open, and she stared down into the bluest eyes she had ever seen. They glazed as if trying to focus, and his forehead wrinkled. He tried to push up, but she restrained him with her hand on his chest.

"Don't move. You've been hurt, but we're going to help you."

He frowned and struggled to speak. "H–h–hurt?"

"Yes, you've been shot, but you're going to be all right." She bit her lip after the words were out. Should she have said that? Her father said he was hurt badly.

Daniel stared up at her for a moment then closed his eyes, and his body relaxed. Terrified that he had died, she leaned over him to see if she could detect breathing. His body jerked, and his eyes blinked open again. He stared at her with eyes that held the wild look of one lost in another world. He tried to raise his arm, but it fell back to his side.

He thrashed his head from side to side on the pillow. "Mama! Where are you, Mama?"

Tears flooded Tave's eyes, and she glanced over her shoulder at her father reentering the room. "He's calling for his mother."

Her father nodded. "I've heard ninety-year-old men call for their mother when they're dying. I suppose one never gets too old to want the comfort a mother can give." He sighed and glanced down at his patient. "Well, let's see if we can save this boy for his mother."

two

Three hours later, Tave put the last of her father's tools away, placed her hands in the small of her back, and stretched. Working with her father hadn't been nearly as bad as she'd thought it would be. Even the blood hadn't made her queasy like it usually did. Maybe she was getting used to being in a doctor's office. Or maybe her calm in surgery had been brought about by the plaintive cry of a man calling out for his mother. Whatever the reason, she felt hopeful that her father had succeeded in saving Daniel Luckett's life.

She stepped to the door of the small bedroom where recuperating patients stayed. The young man lay on the bed where her father, with the help of Mr. Jensen from the livery stable and one of his workers, had moved him after surgery. Some color had returned to his face, and he appeared to be breathing better. He had survived, but her father had warned her the next forty-eight hours would be critical.

Her father stood beside the bed, watching the rise and fall of Daniel's chest. He turned to her, smiled, and held up the object in his hands for her to see. "Did you see what came on the *Montgomery Belle* today?"

Tave nodded and walked over to her father. "Your new stethoscope arrived. I saw it during the surgery, but I didn't want to distract you by saying anything. How does it work?"

He looked at the instrument and smiled. "You've seen my old stethoscope. It's one long tube that stands upright on the patient's chest. Then I had to place my ear at the top of it to

17

hear anything. A lot of doctors have been afraid this new one with two earpieces would confuse them with different sounds in each ear, but it doesn't. It's great, and just in time for a patient who needs all the help he can get."

Her father stuck the ends in his ears, bent over Daniel, and pressed the stethoscope to his chest. Tave waited until her father straightened before she spoke. "How's he doing?"

"Holding his own right now. We'll have to wait and see. He's young and strong. That should help a lot."

Before Tave could reply, the small bell her father had placed over the front door to alert him to arriving patients jingled. She frowned. Who could be arriving so late in the afternoon?

"Anybody here?" A voice from the waiting room called out.

Tave suppressed a giggle at her father's arched eyebrows. He shook his head. "Martha Thompson's come to see what's going on."

"You want me to go talk to her?"

Her father nodded. "If you don't mind. I'll stay here with Daniel."

Tave hurried into the waiting room and closed the door to the bedroom behind her. Martha Thompson stood just inside the front door, a large basket in her hands. "Hello, Martha. What are you doing here? You're not sick, are you?"

Martha's ample frame shook with laughter. She waved a pudgy hand in dismissal. "Landsakes, no. I thought 'bout you and your pa over here a-workin' to take care of that poor boy that got shot, and I knowed you was hungry. I brought you some supper."

Guilt flowed through Tave. Martha might be the biggest gossip in town, but she also had a heart that looked to the needs of her friends. "That's so sweet of you. I haven't had time to fix anything for Poppa and me. He'll be so excited that you stopped by. He always tries to get whatever you cooked when we have the church dinners."

Martha's face flushed, and she lowered her eyelids. "Oh, hush now. You gonna give me the big head. I's just trying to help out a friend in need." She lifted the cloth covering the top of the basket, and the delicious aromas that drifted from it made Tave's stomach growl. "I fixed chicken and dumplings for our supper and had plenty left over. I stuck in a piece of cornbread, too. So you and your pa enjoy it."

Tave took the basket from Martha. "Let me get the bowls out, and you can take your basket home with you."

Martha shook her head. "No need for that. I'll stop by tomorrow and get 'em. That'll give me a chance to see how the young fellow that was shot is doing." Martha glanced toward the closed bedroom door. "How is he doing?"

"He came through surgery. Now it's just wait and see. The next forty-eight hours are critical, Poppa says."

Martha's eyebrows drew down over her nose. "Um, you don't say. Did you find out anything about him? Like where he's from? What made him try to take that gun away from the gambler on the boat?"

"No, Martha. I'm afraid I don't know anything. Just that he's a very sick person right now. We'll all have to pray that he pulls through."

Martha nodded. "I'll be doin' that, and I'll be back tomorrow to check on him."

Tave handed Martha the basket. "I can't thank you enough for the food. I'll have your bowls ready to return tomorrow."

"I'll be back to get them. Maybe you'll know more about him when I come."

Tave tried to suppress the giggle in her throat. "We'll see."

She took Martha by the arm, escorted her to the door, and opened it. "I don't want to keep you from your family, and I should see if Poppa needs me. Thanks again, and you have a good night."

Martha stepped onto the porch and turned. "Like I said, I'll see you—" She stopped midsentence, and a slow smile curled her lips. She tilted her head to one side and glanced at Tave. "Well, would you get a look at who's here. No wonder you're trying to get me to hurry off."

Tave frowned and stepped onto the porch beside Martha. Her heart gave a thump as she spied Matthew Chandler coming around the corner of the building. When he saw her, his dark eyes lit up, and he smiled. Stepping onto the porch, he took off the wide-brimmed hat he wore and nodded to Martha, then Tave.

"Good evening, ladies. It's nice to see you." He turned to Tave. "I didn't expect to find you at your father's office. I thought with the last day of school over, you'd be home resting."

Martha grinned. "She don't have time to rest. Not with all that's happened around here today." She reached out and patted Tave's hand. "Well, I know when I need to leave two young people alone. I'll see you tomorrow, Tave."

Tave shook her head and chuckled as Martha walked down the steps and turned in the direction of her home. "That woman never ceases to amaze me. She comes over here to get all the news on my father's latest patient, but she brings us supper. You can't help loving her."

Matthew nodded. "I know. But what did she mean about all that's happened today?"

"Come on inside, and I'll tell you."

Matthew followed her into the building, and she related

the events that had caused Daniel Luckett to become her father's patient. "At the moment, he's fighting for his life."

Matthew picked up a medical book that lay on a table and flipped to the first page. "That's too bad, but I'm sure he'll be all right. Those deckhands are a resourceful bunch. Not very intelligent, but hardy, if you know what I mean."

An uneasy feeling rippled through her at the unconcerned tone of Matthew's voice. She was just about to say that she didn't know what he meant when the door to the bedroom opened.

Her father emerged. "Matthew, what are you doing here so late in the day? Not sick I hope."

Matthew dropped the book on the table and shook his head. "No, I'm fine. It's one of my tenant farmers, Sam Perry. He almost cut his fingers off this afternoon when he was chopping wood."

Her father looked around. "Why didn't you bring him with you? Wasn't he able to come to town?"

Matthew laughed. "Oh yes. He's with me. I had him wait out back until I told you he was here. I didn't figure you wanted him waiting inside."

Her father's eyes narrowed, and he glared at Matthew. "Waiting outside with his fingers almost cut off? What were you thinking?"

Tave's heart dropped to the pit of her stomach, but Matthew shrugged and smiled at her father. "I know you talk about your oath to help everybody, Dr. Spencer, but this is a black man. The people in this town don't let black people walk through their front doors, and they sure don't want to share a waiting room with them."

Her father clenched his fists and took a step toward Matthew. "Now listen here, young man—"

Tave grabbed her father's arm. "Let's not waste time arguing, Poppa. A hurt man sitting outside needs some help."

Her father took a deep breath, walked to the back door, and flung it open. "Sam," he called out. "Come on in here, and let me look at your hand."

A black man Tave had seen in town several times shuffled through the back door. A bloody rag bound the injured hand. He didn't look up as her father steered him into the exam room. She took a step forward. "Do you need me, Poppa?"

He gritted his teeth and shook his head. "Not now. Keep Matthew company."

After her father and Sam had disappeared, Matthew walked over and stopped next to her. "I'm sorry I haven't had a chance to see you this week, but we've been busy. Things should slow down in a few weeks. I'll make it up to you then."

Tave stared up into the dark eyes that had attracted her to Matthew when she and her father had first come to Willow Bend from eastern Tennessee eight years before. She'd been only twelve at the time, and she'd thought the nineteen-year-old Matthew Chandler was the most handsome man she'd ever seen, and the richest.

He had hardly noticed her then, but that had all changed a year ago when he suddenly developed an interest in the young woman she'd become. He'd been a steady visitor at their home ever since, but on many nights, her father, who'd supported the Union in the war, and Matthew, a staunch supporter of the Confederate cause, had clashed.

She wondered sometimes if they would ever be able to find some common ground in their beliefs. But then, that seemed to be the problem of many people in this part of Alabama. She tried to tell her father that Matthew was a product of his upbringing, but it hadn't changed his opinion of Matthew.

Tave, however, had come to the conclusion that Matthew had many likeable qualities, and when he and her father weren't arguing, she enjoyed his company. As she'd told Savannah earlier, she wasn't getting any younger, and no other young men had come calling.

She smiled at Matthew. "I'll look forward to seeing you more."

&

The clock in her father's office chimed midnight. Tave shivered in the dark room where she sat beside Daniel's bed and pulled the quilt around her body. She didn't know if there was a chill in the air or if she shivered with concern for the unconscious man. Her father had done all he could to save Daniel's life. Now it was up to God.

The oil lamp on the table beside her flickered and cast shadows on the wall by Daniel's bed. He'd been restless for the past few hours, but her father had warned her he would be so soon after surgery. If Daniel lived through the night, he would have a good chance of survival, her father had said.

A moan drifted from the bed. Tave jumped to her feet and felt his forehead. Perspiration covered his brow. Wringing out the cloth she'd kept in a bowl of water, she laid it on his forehead.

His head twitched on the pillow, and his hand jerked the cloth from his head. "No, don't do it!"

Tave gasped in surprise at the shouted words. She reached for the lamp and held it up to see if his eyes were open, but they weren't. He groaned again, and she set the lamp down and repositioned the cloth.

His mouth opened, and his body shook. "Leave her alone!" The shout cut through the silent room like thunder.

Tave reached for his hand and wrapped both of hers around it. "It's all right. I'm here with you."

He took a deep breath, but he continued to tremble. A whimper escaped his throat. "Mama, come back. Don't leave me."

For the second time, Tave heard the unconscious man call for his mother, and it touched her heart. She wondered what had happened to his mother and why he called out to her. Tave thought of her own mother, who'd died when she was five years old. Sometimes she had trouble remembering what her mother looked like, but she had never overcome the emptiness of not having her in her life.

Still holding Daniel's hand, Tave dropped to her knees beside his bed and bowed her head. "Dear God, I pray You will calm this man's heart and give him peace for tonight. Let him sleep so that his body may begin to heal. Only You know what causes his heart to ache so, Lord, and I pray You'll ease his pain."

Tave lost track of time as she continued to pray, but the longer she stayed on her knees, the quieter Daniel became. Only when his body relaxed and a soft snore echoed through the room did she rise.

She stared at the handsome young man who'd come so close to death and thanked God again for sparing his life. Then she sat back down in the chair and wrapped the quilt around her.

As she huddled beside the soft light from the lamp, she thought about Daniel's earlier cries and wondered what they meant. Maybe something had happened in his past that had left him deeply scarred. Her father had often told her that wounds to the spirit can be much worse than those inflicted on the body. Perhaps God wanted her father and her to help heal Daniel's spirit, too. Only time would tell.

three

Daniel Luckett drifted in a dream world. Time held no meaning. At some point, he'd heard voices. He didn't know who the people were, but something in his soul told him they were discussing him. Snatches of sentences came to him: *saved my life. . .lost a lot of blood. . .we're going to help you.* He didn't know what any of it meant, but the last one comforted him.

We're going to help you. The voice that spoke those words had sounded like music. It had the same lyrical quality of the songs his mother used to sing. She could always make him feel better, just as that soft angelic sound had.

Who was with him? At times it seemed like many people, and at other times just the comforting voice. It would come to him at odd times, telling him to open his mouth or prodding him to turn his body. Sometimes he could hear a soft whisper beside his bed, as if someone knelt beside him and prayed, and he would strain to open his eyes. But it was no use. His eyes felt glued shut. Just when he would think he was going to be victorious and catch a glimpse of the illusive spirit who hovered over him, quiet would return. And with it, he would descend back into his dream world.

How long he'd drifted like this, he didn't know. He had to wake up. He needed to know what had happened to him.

A groan echoed in his mind, and he wondered if the sound came from his mouth or if it only resonated in his mind. With all the strength he could summon, he blinked. His eyes opened.

He lay still for a moment. Then he rubbed his fingers on the blanket that covered him. The touch was unfamiliar. He turned his head to the left and saw the outline of a window. Beyond the pane, he could only see darkness.

Turning his head to the right, his eyes grew wider. A round table sat a few feet away from the bed where he lay. An oil lamp on top cast an eerie glow across the room. But it wasn't the light that took his breath away. It was the woman in the chair next to the table.

She slept soundly, her auburn hair loose and tumbling over her shoulders. She wore a shapeless, blue housedress with long sleeves and a high neckline. He struggled to focus his eyes on the sleeping woman. His heart pounded. He had never seen anyone more beautiful in his life.

She stirred and opened her eyes. They stared at each other, but then she smiled and jumped to her feet. "Oh, you're awake. I've been waiting for that to happen."

He tried to speak, but his mouth was dry as cotton. "W–water," he whispered.

She picked up a pitcher, poured some water into a glass, and stepped to the side of his bed. Slipping one arm beneath his head, she lifted him up just enough to get his lips on the glass. He sipped at the water until she pulled the glass away from his mouth.

"Not too much just yet. I don't want you getting sick."

He fell back against the pillow and groaned. It surprised him how the little amount of energy he'd exerted had completely tired him. He swallowed and glanced up at the beautiful woman who leaned over him. Her long hair swung close to his face, and he reached toward it.

She didn't flinch as his fingers touched the tip of her hair and caressed a soft curl between his fingers. "Your hair is beautiful."

She chuckled, wrapped her fingers around his hand, and guided it back to the bed. "And you're still delirious."

Daniel glanced around. Was he imagining this beautiful creature? He frowned. "Where am I?"

"You're at my father's office. He's the doctor in Willow Bend."

He tried to turn on his side, and pain surged through his body. "Wh–what happened to me?"

"You were shot on board the *Montgomery Belle*. Do you remember anything?"

He thought for a moment, and he recalled going into a cabin with Captain Hawkins. What happened next seemed fuzzy in his memory. He shook his head. "No."

She tucked the covers around him. "That's all right. It will all come back to you."

"How long have I been here?"

"Three days."

Daniel raised a hand to his forehead and rubbed. "Have you been with me all that time?"

She smiled again. "Either my father or I have been. But you don't need to worry about anything right now. You need to rest."

"Wait," he called out as she turned to go back to her chair. "What's your name?"

She smiled down at him. "Tave Spencer."

Daniel closed his eyes. "Tave Spencer." The name slid like velvet across his tongue and spilled from his mouth. It reminded him of the words of the ballads his mother used to sing. Tave Spencer—a poetic name with the soothing effect of a lullaby. He'd never heard anything lovelier in his life.

He closed his eyes and slept.

❧

Daniel awoke to the sound of birds chirping. He remembered

seeing a window when he'd awakened once before, and he turned his head in that direction. Sunlight streamed through the panes and cast dancing rays across the patchwork quilt that covered his body. He lay still and listened to the noisy twittering outside.

A memory of touching silky curls returned, and he smiled at the name he'd dreamed about. *Tave Spencer*, that's what she'd said. He glanced at the chair where she'd sat, but it was empty.

He had no idea if it was morning or afternoon. From the busy sounds outside the window, he suspected it was morning. If it was, he wondered where the woman he'd spoken with had gone. Or maybe she'd been a dream. He couldn't be sure.

The door to the room opened, and a man walked in. His brown eyes lit up, and he smiled as he walked toward Daniel's bed. He stopped beside him and peered over the top of the wire-rimmed spectacles perched on his nose. "Well, you're finally awake. I thought you might rejoin us this morning."

Through narrowed eyes, Daniel studied the man, but he couldn't recall having ever seen him before. "Do I know you?"

"I'm Dr. Spencer. I've been taking care of you for the past few days."

Daniel thought of the woman he'd seen and looked past the doctor, but she was nowhere in sight. "There was a woman here."

Dr. Spencer nodded. "My daughter, Tave. She's been helping me look after you." He pressed his fingers to Daniel's wrist and pulled out a pocket watch. He stared at the watch for what seemed an eternity before he smiled and released his hold. "Your pulse is much better. I think you're on the road to recovery."

Daniel tried to lift his head, but the room rotated as a

wave of dizziness washed over him. He sank back against the pillow and gasped. "What day is it?"

"Today is Monday. We brought you here last Friday from the *Montgomery Belle*. Do you remember anything?"

Daniel closed his eyes and concentrated. "I remember going with Captain Hawkins into a cabin. There was a card game." He opened his eyes. "There's nothing else until I woke up and saw your daughter."

Dr. Spencer pointed to Daniel's side. "One of the gamblers threatened Captain Hawkins with a gun, and you tried to wrestle it from him. You ended up being shot, but you probably saved the captain's life. He's very thankful, but he was concerned for you. The boat went on to Montgomery, but he said he'd check on you when they returned."

"Captain Hawkins is a good man."

"That he is." Dr. Spencer pointed to Daniel's side. "I need to check on your wound."

Daniel gritted his teeth and tried not to moan as the doctor pulled the quilt back and probed at his side. After a few minutes, Dr. Spencer covered him up and stepped away.

"How am I doing?" Daniel asked.

Dr. Spencer pulled the chair up to the bedside and sat down. "I think you're a mighty lucky young man that the bullet didn't do a lot of internal damage. There was some damage to an artery. That's what caused you to lose so much blood, but I was able to repair that. You should be up and around in a few days."

Daniel heaved a sigh of relief. "Thank you, Dr. Spencer, for all you've done for me." He bit down on his lip. "I don't have any money right now, but I'll pay you as soon as I recover enough to get on up to Montgomery. I'd planned to leave the *Montgomery Belle* and take a job on the docks there."

Dr. Spencer waved his hand in dismissal. "Don't worry about what you owe me, son. Captain Hawkins said he'd take care of everything. Like I said, he's mighty thankful to be alive."

"And so am I." Daniel glanced around the room. "How long do you think I'll be here?"

"Well, that depends on how soon you get your strength back. I'd say—"

A rustling at the door caught their attention, and Daniel and Dr. Spencer glanced in that direction. Daniel's heart pounded in his chest at the sight of the woman with the auburn hair. "Oh, you're awake again." She glided into the room and stopped beside her father's chair. "He looks much better, doesn't he, Poppa?"

Her father chuckled and pushed up from where he sat. "He only had one way to go." He glanced back at Daniel. "I don't mind telling you, son, when you were brought in here, I didn't think you had a chance of living. Glad to see I was wrong."

Tave looped her arm through her father's and smiled at him. "That's because he had a wonderful doctor to take care of him."

Pride showed in her father's eyes as he stared at her. "And a great nurse to coax him back to the land of the living."

Tave stretched on her tiptoes and kissed her father on the cheek. The love between the two was obvious. It reminded Daniel of his mother and how close they had been. There wasn't a day that went by that he didn't think of her and how much he missed her.

He cleared his throat. "I want to thank both of you for what you've done for me." He glanced at Tave. "It meant a lot to me when I woke up and saw you in the room. I knew I wasn't alone."

Dr. Spencer smiled. "I keep telling her she'd make a fine nurse, but she's bound and determined to teach school."

Daniel frowned. "So you're a teacher. Why aren't you there today?"

A soft peal of laughter from her lips stirred his blood, and he stared at this woman he'd first seen in the darkness of his room. What was it about her that excited him? Perhaps it was gratitude for what she had done for him, but something told him it was more.

"School is out for the summer."

Daniel nodded. "Yeah, it is that time of year again."

A bell tinkled in another room, and Dr. Spencer sighed. "I suppose that's a patient. I'll be back to check on you, Daniel."

Tave watched her father leave the room before she faced Daniel again. "So, are you hungry? I made some broth this morning. You need to eat something."

"Have I eaten since I've been here?"

She nodded. "Yes. I'm afraid at times I had to force you, but I did get liquids down you."

The memory of someone forcing a spoon into his mouth returned, and he grinned. "So you're the one who tortured me when all I wanted to do was sleep."

Her eyes held a mischievous glint, and she crossed her arms. "Guilty as charged, but at least you didn't die from hunger."

The realization of how close he'd come to death hit him, and he swallowed the sudden flash of fear that filled his throat. "No, I didn't die. And for that I owe your father and you a great debt of gratitude. Thank you, Tave, for taking care of me."

A crimson flush spread across her face. "You remembered my name. I didn't think you were conscious enough to know what I said to you."

His gaze strayed to the bun on top of her head and recalled how her hair had cascaded around her shoulders. He wished he could pull the pins from her head and let the curls tumble free again. He swallowed and tried to smile. "I remember."

She stared at him for a moment before she reached down and smoothed the apron that covered her dress. For a fleeting moment he believed he saw her hands tremble, but he dismissed the thought. She backed toward the door. "I'll be right back with something for you to eat."

He smiled. "Take your time. I guess I'll be in this same spot when you get back. I'm not going anywhere today."

After she hurried from the room, he settled back on his pillow and smiled. The lines from a ballad his mother used to sing drifted into his mind, and he tried to recall the words. He hummed the melody, but the exact words wouldn't come. They were about a beautiful woman who was peerless in beauty and even a prince could find no sweeter creature.

From what he'd seen of Tave Spencer so far, she could very well have been the inspiration for those words.

❧

An hour later Tave removed the napkin she'd draped around Daniel's neck and laid it on the tray with the remains of his meal. She propped her hands on her hips and stared down at Daniel, whose head she'd elevated with two pillows. "Do you want to lie flat, or do you want to keep the pillows?"

"I think I'll stay like this for a while."

"Okay." She bent to pick up the tray but turned when his hand touched her arm. "Do you want something else?"

"Where are you going?"

"I'm going to take these back to the other room. Then I thought I'd let you rest."

He shook his head. "I haven't done anything but sleep for days. Would you mind coming back and talking with me?"

"I'd be glad to keep you company. With school out, I'm helping my father here anyway." Her eyes twinkled. "And right now, you're my favorite patient. Of course that may change if we get someone else in here."

He laughed. "Maybe I can endear myself to you."

She picked up the tray and carried it into the small room in the back of the building that they used for a kitchen from time to time when her father had to keep a close watch on a patient. A woodstove stood against one wall, and a table and two chairs sat in the middle of the room. A pie safe containing the remains of an apple cobbler Martha Thompson had brought the day before rested against the other wall.

Tave smiled at how well she and her father had eaten since Daniel's mishap with the gambler on board the *Montgomery Belle.* Martha had arrived every day with some new dish in an effort to help with their meals. Although Tave appreciated the thoughtfulness, she knew Martha's main motive had been to glean news about their mysterious patient.

Tave set the tray on the table and dropped into one of the chairs. She rubbed her eyes and yawned. For the last three nights, she'd sat beside Daniel Luckett's bed. Although she'd dozed some, she could feel the results of not sleeping in her own bed. Maybe tonight she could leave Daniel and go home. In his office, her father had a sofa he slept on when he had a patient, so he would be here in case Daniel needed something.

Still, she didn't like the idea of leaving Daniel without someone close by. Her father could be a sound sleeper sometimes, and Daniel might be unable to wake him. Maybe she'd stay another night.

Her eyes grew wide at a sudden realization that flashed

into her mind. She had developed a protective feeling toward Daniel that she'd never felt with anyone else before. Perhaps it stemmed from how she had cared for him after surgery, or it could be the memory of his calling for his mother. The fear she'd heard in his voice had pricked her heart. It reminded her of the children she taught and how they wanted their mothers when they fell and hurt themselves.

Her father had once told her that he felt like a protector of the people he cared for. Maybe that's all it was with her. Soon Daniel would be recovered, and he would leave with Captain Hawkins on the *Montgomery Belle*. He would be just another patient to her father, but she knew he would always be special to her. After all, Daniel was her miracle. From the moment her father had first seen Daniel, he had thought the man would die. When she'd seen his pale face, she'd thought so, too. Until a small voice had whispered in her heart that God wasn't finished with this young man.

Some might say she was imagining she heard the voice of God, but Tave knew differently. Daniel needed more than the skill of a surgeon's knife to heal his body. He needed the touch of the Father to repair something much deadlier. She didn't know what Daniel Luckett had experienced in his life. All she knew was that God had told her to pray, and that's what she'd done.

For the last three nights, she'd knelt by his bed and prayed that God would spare him and heal whatever damage life had inflicted. Daniel had lived. Now maybe God would show her what else she needed to do.

four

A week later, Tave held on to Daniel's arm as she helped him through the front door and onto the small porch of her father's office. She guided him to a rocking chair that sat in the corner of the porch and helped him ease down into it, then took a step back and smiled at the excitement on his face.

"How does it feel to be outside again?"

"It makes me think I'm really going to recover." He closed his eyes and inhaled. "Ah, is that honeysuckle I smell?"

Tave nodded and dropped down into a chair beside Daniel. "Yes. We have honeysuckle climbing up a trellis on the other side of the building." She inhaled. "I love the smell of it at this time of year before it gets so hot it's hard to breathe."

He settled back in his chair and glanced up and down the street. "So this is what Willow Bend looks like at street level. The *Montgomery Belle* stopped here a lot when I was working on her, but I never got off and came ashore. This is my first chance to get a close look."

Tave smiled ruefully. "I'm sorry you almost had to die to see how we live."

His gaze drifted over her, and his blue eyes twinkled. "If I'd known there was such a pretty nurse living just over the bluff, I imagine I would have been to see you before now."

Her face warmed, and she averted her gaze. "I'm afraid you wouldn't have found me here. I would have been at school or at home."

He sighed. "Just my luck. By the way, where is home? I suppose for the first few days I thought you and your father lived in back of his office. Now that you've deserted me at night to go home, I realize you have a house somewhere else."

"My father and I live in a house at the edge of town. We moved into it when we first settled here. It's small, but it meets our needs."

He swiveled in his chair and stared at her. "Then you haven't lived here all your life?"

"No. My father has a friend who is a doctor over in Selma, and he told us about Willow Bend needing a doctor. So Poppa decided it would be a good place to live. We came when I was twelve."

"And what about your mother?"

"She died when I was a child. We lived in Knoxville. Then when the war came, Poppa served with the Union Army as a doctor. I stayed with my grandmother. After the war, we came to Alabama. We've never been sorry, except Poppa clashes a lot with the residents around here when the war is mentioned."

Daniel chuckled. "I'll bet he does."

She tilted her head and stared at him. "And what about you? Where did you grow up?"

He stared toward the bluff and didn't answer for a moment. When he did, Tave could detect a tremor in his voice. "I guess you could say I'm from Ohio. At least that's where I was born and lived for sixteen years. But I've traveled around so much in the last seven years I could call a lot of places home."

Tave thought of how he called out for his mother when he was so ill. "Are your parents still in Ohio?"

He shook his head. "I was six years old when my pa joined an Ohio regiment and went off to fight in the war. He died less than a year later at Shiloh. We moved in with my mother's brother for a while, but his wife and children didn't want us there. When the man on the next farm asked my mother to marry him, she did. She figured we'd have a home, and we wouldn't be a burden on her brother anymore."

The wistful tone of his voice told Tave that Daniel's memories were very difficult for him to discuss. She placed her hand on his arm. "You love your mother very much, don't you?"

He stared down at her hand for a moment. When he looked up, a moist sheen covered his eyes. "I did. She died when I was sixteen."

"Is that why you left home?"

"Yes." Daniel's mouth thinned into a straight line, and he tried to push up from his chair. "I'm getting tired. Maybe I've had enough fresh air for now."

Tave jumped to her feet and grasped his arm. "Let me help you."

As Daniel straightened to his full height, his face grew pale, and his knees started to buckle. He swayed toward her. "I. . .I f–feel d–dizzy."

She threw her arms around him and eased him back into the chair. When he was seated again, she dropped to her knees and stared at him. "Are you all right? Do you want me to get you some water?"

Perspiration dotted his head, and he wiped his hand across his face. "I'm okay now. I think I tried to get up too fast. Let me rest for a minute."

"I think I need to get my father." She glanced at him once more before she ran to the door. "Poppa, I need you out here."

Her father came hurrying from his office. "What's the matter?"

"Daniel's dizzy, and I need some help getting him back inside."

Her father's lips thinned into a grim line. Getting on one side of Daniel, he motioned for Tave to take his other arm. When they had Daniel back on his feet, they steered him toward the door.

As they crossed the porch, Daniel glanced from one to the other. "I'm all right. There's no need for all this fuss."

Her father reached out to open the door. "We're not making a fuss. Just taking precautions. I didn't save your life to have you fall and crack your skull. Now, I think you've been up quite long enough for one day."

A footstep sounded on the porch behind them, and Tave glanced over her shoulder. Matthew stood there, his gaze flitting over the three of them.

"Do you need my help, Dr. Spencer?" he asked.

Her father glanced back. "Oh hello, Matthew. We're getting this young man back to bed. Are you here to see me or Tave?"

"Actually, I'm here to speak with Tave."

Tave nodded toward the inside of the office. "Then come on in, and I'll be right with you."

She and her father held on to Daniel's arms as they eased their way across the floor and into the patient bedroom. When he was in bed once more, Daniel smiled up at them. "Thanks. I guess I'm not as strong as I thought."

Tave glanced at her father. "Do you need me, or can I go talk to Matthew?"

He waved his hand in dismissal. "Go on." He cocked his eyebrow and glanced up at Tave. "Doesn't he call on you enough at home without having to come here, too?"

Tave shook her head in dismay. "Poppa, you know you like Matthew."

Dr. Spencer shrugged. "I guess I'll have to like him if you

do. Now go on and see what he wants."

Tave opened her mouth to protest her father's words, but the look on Daniel's face made her heart plummet to the pit of her stomach. His blue eyes no longer held the twinkle she'd seen earlier. They'd clouded, and deep lines cut into his cheeks as he bit down on his lip.

She stepped closer to the bed. "Are you in pain, Daniel?"

His chest heaved, and he closed his eyes. "Don't worry about me. I'm just tired." The words had a lifeless quality.

She glanced up at her father. "Do you think sitting on the porch was too much for him? I didn't mean to keep him out so long."

Her father frowned. "Maybe it was. I'll check him out and see." He glanced toward the other room where Matthew waited. "Now you go on. I'll let you know."

Tave backed away from the bed. "Call me if you need me."

She walked to the door and turned to stare back at Daniel. He lay on his back with his eyes closed. He didn't move as her father bent over him and examined the wound in his side. For a moment when she'd stared into Daniel's eyes, she'd been frightened. She'd caught a glimpse of the same look she'd seen when he had called for his mother.

Perhaps he was sorry he'd spoken of his past life today. She'd learned very little, though, and she had the feeling that there was still much Daniel hadn't told her. If it was going to upset him, maybe she didn't need to probe too much into his past. All she could do was pray that he could find some peace.

She pasted a big smile on her face and headed toward the room where Matthew waited.

As she walked through the door, his gazed flitted over her body. The scrutiny in his eyes made her face warm, and she brushed at her hair. "I'm surprised to see you today, Matthew."

He strode across the floor and stopped beside her. "I know. I don't usually drop by during the day, but I came to tell you something."

She gazed up at him. "What is it?"

"I'm going away for several weeks."

His words shocked her. "Going away? Where?"

"You know my mother's sister lives on Dauphin Island near Mobile. She's wanted my mother to visit for a long time, but there never seemed to be time. Now things have slowed down some with the spring planting, and it's a good time to leave. Pa doesn't get along with my mother's family, so he wants me to accompany her downriver. I'll be gone for about six weeks."

Tave wondered why she didn't feel any sadness at the thought of Matthew being gone for such a length of time. Her gaze strayed to the doorway that led to the room where Daniel lay. The thought crossed her mind that his presence might have something to do with her lack of feeling about Matthew's departure. She smiled up at Matthew. "I'll miss you, but I'm glad your mother will get to be with her sister."

A puzzled look crossed his face, and he frowned. "You're not upset that I'll be gone for so long?"

"Why would I be upset? I understand you have obligations to your family."

He stepped closer, and his dark gaze bored into her. "I'm glad you understand how important my family is to me, Tave, but I have other needs in my life besides my parents and preserving the heritage of Winterville."

"What kind of needs?"

"I'm ready to take a wife, a woman who can share my life with me on the land that's been in my family for generations."

He reached for her hand, brought it to his lips, and kissed it. Straightening, he stared into her eyes. "You're a wonderful woman, Tave. When I come back, I want to speak to your father. I think it's time we decided about our future together."

"Our future?" She knew the words came from her mouth, but they sounded very much like the nighttime croak of the frogs on the pond behind their house.

He nodded. "After everything is finalized, I'd like for you and your father to accompany my parents and me to the St. James Hotel in Selma for a few nights. We can celebrate our engagement with our families, and you and my mother can visit the shops in town to pick out your trousseau. I'd love to show you the hotel. The view of the river from the balcony is beautiful."

"The St. James?" Tave's heart pounded in her chest. She'd asked her father several times to take her there, but they'd never been able to afford it. Yet this wasn't a trip to be taken lightly. There were decisions to be made first. "I—I don't know, Matthew. Let's talk about all this when you get back."

He released her hand and smiled. "You can count on our talking about it. I'm a determined man, and I always get what I want."

Tave's breath caught in her throat at the intense look in his dark eyes. He was such a handsome man, but in her mind, Matthew's features dissolved, and another's took their place —one with wheat-colored hair and the deepest blue eyes she'd ever seen.

How could that be? She'd known Daniel less than two weeks, yet already he'd found a special place in her heart. It was probably because she'd come to feel so protective of him. It couldn't be more. She knew nothing about the man who cried out in agony when he was delirious.

She had to concentrate on Matthew, who could offer her a life like she'd never imagined. But did she want it? She dismissed her doubts and smiled. "Come to see us when you get back."

⁂

Daniel heard the front door of the building close, and he supposed Tave's caller had left. His mind still reeled at what he'd heard. Tave was interested in another man. He closed his eyes and tried to swallow the lump that formed in his throat. He should have known. A beautiful woman like her could have any man she wanted.

How foolish he'd been. Day after day, he'd lain in this bed and waited for her to step into his room and smile at him. Her presence was what had pulled him through the dark nights when he felt like he was going to die. She'd brought him back from the dead, and he'd thought it was because she felt a connection to him.

He'd known the moment he saw her sitting in the chair beside his bed that she was different from any other woman he'd ever known. She was the first person he'd ever talked to about his mother. And all the time he'd been thinking about Tave, she'd been in love with someone else.

Daniel lay still until Dr. Spencer finished his examination, pulled the covers back over him, and sat down in a chair next to the bed. "You gave me a fright, young man. I feared you had an infection setting up, but I don't see any evidence of it. What happened to you?"

Daniel reached behind his head and punched his pillow with his fist. "I guess I was just tired. I'm sorry to cause you trouble."

Dr. Spencer laughed. "Trouble? Son, that's what I'm here for. I want to make sure nothing happens to cause you problems down the road."

Daniel glanced at the man who'd worked so hard to save his life, and his heart pricked at the doctor's tired eyes. Patients had come and gone all week, and many times Dr. Spencer had been summoned to go to some farm along the river. He'd never heard the man complain or resist going where he was needed.

There was a peace about Dr. Spencer that Daniel didn't understand. Tave had it, too. He recalled hearing her pray beside his bed, and he realized there was someone else who had once had that same peace—his mother. She'd trusted God all her life, but in the end, it hadn't done her any good.

Daniel pushed the unwelcome thoughts from his head. "I don't know how I can ever repay you for what you and Tave have done for me."

"I'm glad I could help, and I'm also glad Tave has been here. She's been a lifesaver for me. It's hard to take care of patients in the daytime if you're up all night. It's helped me a lot to have her keeping watch over you at night."

Daniel thought of the man he'd seen on the porch. "What did you say Tave's friend's name is?"

A slight frown creased Dr. Spencer's forehead. "That's Matthew Chandler."

Daniel licked his lips and swallowed. "Are they engaged?"

Dr. Spencer shook his head. "Not yet, but I suspect he'll propose soon. Matthew's been calling on Tave for the last year, but he doesn't seem to be in any hurry about getting married." He shrugged. "Maybe I'm wrong. At least I hope I am."

The words surprised Daniel, and he lifted his head. "Don't you want Tave to marry?"

"Of course I do, but I want it to be the right man. Somehow I don't think Matthew's the one. His family is the richest in the county, and he's a nice enough fellow, I guess, although we have some disagreements about the place of former slaves in Alabama life. But then, Dante Rinaldi and I are in the minority when it comes to their rights."

Daniel sank back on his pillow and thought of his father. "I guess you need to add one more to your list. My father died at Shiloh fighting for the Union."

Dr. Spencer's eyes took on a faraway look. "I was there as a doctor with the Union forces. There were horrible losses on both sides. I never will forget a pond that was there. During the fighting, men from both sides came to it so they could drink and bathe their wounds. Many of them and their horses died in that pond. By the end of the day it was red with blood." He closed his eyes for a moment, and his lips trembled. "The Bloody Pond, that's what they still call it."

Daniel reached out and touched Dr. Spencer's arm. "I'd like to think you were with my father when he died that day."

Dr. Spencer patted Daniel's hand and pushed to his feet. "I don't know. I could have been. I saw enough death that day to last me the rest of my life."

"You must be talking about Shiloh."

They both glanced toward the door where Tave stood. Her father exhaled and nodded. "Yes, but the day's too beautiful to talk about such sad topics. I think I'll go over to Mr. Perkins's store and see how he's doing."

He moved to the door but stopped when a musical rumble drifted from the direction of the river. Tave smiled up at her father. "That must be the *Montgomery Belle*."

Dr. Spencer glanced back at Daniel. "I guess you'll be having a visitor soon. Captain Hawkins said he'd come to see you when they returned."

Daniel pushed up on his elbows. "Maybe he'll let me rejoin the crew for the trip downriver."

Tave gasped and rushed to his bedside. "Don't you even think about it. You need to stay here longer to regain your strength." She turned to her father. "Tell him, Poppa. He can't leave yet."

Dr. Spencer shook his head. "You're not ready to go. Give it a few more weeks. Captain Hawkins will make a return trip to Montgomery, and you can leave then."

Daniel sank back on his pillow. "Very well. I'll give it a few more weeks."

Tave bent over and tucked the quilt around him. "That's better. Now let's not hear anything else about your leaving before you've completely healed." She straightened and smiled down at him. "I'm going to fix some tea for you and Captain Hawkins to enjoy while he's here."

As she hurried from the room, Daniel's heart thudded. How could he stay this close to her for another few weeks, knowing that she was in love with someone else? She'd awakened something in him that he thought long dead, and he couldn't bear the thought of her marrying another man. As soon as Dr. Spencer released him, he was going to head for Montgomery and leave Tave Spencer far behind.

five

Tave knew something was wrong. Daniel had spoken very little since Captain Hawkins had come to see him earlier. With this being his first night to sit at the kitchen table for supper, she had expected a more lively conversation. Instead, Daniel had hardly spoken, and she and her father had spent most of the time discussing the yield she hoped to get from her vegetable garden this spring.

The silence from Daniel began to grate on her nerves, and she stared at him. He glanced up then diverted his gaze back to his plate. He shoveled the last bite of his fried peach pie in his mouth and picked up his coffee cup.

Tave pushed at the last bite of pie on her plate with her fork. "The lady who's been bringing us so much food since you've been ill made these pies."

Daniel took a sip of coffee and nodded. "I'll have to thank her."

Tave waited for him to say something else. When he didn't, she reached across the table, picked up Daniel's empty plate, and stacked it on top of hers and her father's. "I noticed when Captain Hawkins came today he brought all your belongings from the boat."

Daniel nodded. "He said they were in such a hurry to depart the day I was shot that they forgot all about getting my clothes to me." He glanced at Dr. Spencer. "I appreciate you finding me something to wear in the meantime."

The doctor set his coffee cup down and wiped his mouth on his napkin. "No problem. The ladies of the church took care of that. I always call on them when a patient has a need, and they never disappoint me."

"I hope I get to meet them so I can thank them."

Her father chuckled. "Oh, I imagine when word gets out that you're better, they'll all be flocking around." His eyes twinkled. "Several of them have unmarried daughters."

Tave swatted at her father's arm. "Stop it, Poppa. You're embarrassing Daniel."

"Well, I don't want to do that." Dr. Spencer straightened in his chair and turned toward Daniel. "How was your visit with Captain Hawkins?"

Daniel took a sip of coffee and set the cup down. "Fine, I guess."

Tave's father glanced at Daniel. "You guess?"

Daniel leaned back in his chair and sighed. "He gave me some bad news."

Tave set the dishes in the dry sink and sank back into her chair. "What kind of bad news?"

"The *Montgomery Belle* needs some repairs. He probably won't be coming back this way until fall, if then. The company is sending him to New Orleans to work until the *Belle* is ready to go again."

Her father nodded. "He told me that. But why is that bad news?"

"Because it means I'll have to delay going on to Montgomery."

Her father pushed back from the table and stood up. "Not necessarily. There are other boats that stop at Willow Bend. You can go on one of them—when you're well enough, that is."

Daniel picked up his spoon and stirred the coffee in his cup. "I don't have the money for a ticket. I could work on the *Belle*, but there probably wouldn't be a job on another ship. I've been thinking about what to do. Maybe when I'm stronger, I can find some kind of job around here, just temporary of course, and make enough money to get me up to Montgomery."

Tave put her elbows on the table and crossed her arms. "I think that's a good idea. We can help you look for something." She glanced at her father. "Isn't Mr. Perkins always talking about how he needs someone to help in the store?"

"He is. I'll talk to him in the morning." Her father's eyes narrowed, and he studied Daniel for a moment. "If you continue to improve as much as you have this past week, it shouldn't be too long before you could do some light work. Maybe sweeping up, helping customers, that sort of stuff."

Daniel smiled, and Tave was struck once again by how his eyes crinkled at the corners when he smiled. She reached across the table and patted his arm. "Then that's all settled. Now why don't you two go into the other room while I wash the dishes?"

Her father turned to leave, but Daniel reached out and stopped him. "There's something else. I'll need a place to stay. Is there somebody around town who has a room I could use in exchange for doing odd jobs for them?"

Her father clapped his hand on Daniel's back. "Son, you have a place to stay as long as you're in Willow Bend. That bed in the other room is yours as long as you need it."

"But what if you have another patient who needs to stay here?"

"We'll take care of that if it happens. Let's just leave all this in the Lord's hands for now. Since you're feeling better, I think it's time for Tave and me to go back home to sleep. You stay here, but we expect you to be at our house for meals. Is that all right with you?"

"That sounds good to me. Thank you, Dr. Spencer. You and Captain Hawkins have been better to me than anybody else ever has."

Her father chuckled. "It's easy to be good to nice people, Daniel, and I can tell you're a fine young man. Now I'm going to work on my accounts. Why don't you stay and keep Tave company until she has to leave?"

Tave watched her father walk through the door before she glanced back at Daniel. "You can talk to me while I wash dishes."

He pushed up from his chair and steadied his legs that appeared to wobble. "I may still be a little weak, but I can help, if that's all right."

She laughed and carried her cup to the dry sink. "I never turn down an offer of help." She set the cup down and reached for the apron she'd hung on a peg by the stove before supper. She glanced over her shoulder and smiled at Daniel. His hair that tumbled over his forehead reminded her of how different he was from Matthew, who was always perfectly groomed. The way they looked, though, wasn't the only difference between the two men.

Matthew didn't have to worry about money. Daniel did, but the fact that he wanted to earn his way made her respect him. There was a lot to like about Daniel Luckett, and she was glad he was going to be in Willow Bend longer.

૨઼

Daniel couldn't take his eyes off Tave. She turned from the dry sink and smiled at him, and he thought his chest would burst from the pounding of his heart. He needed to get away from Willow Bend. He was a drifter, a man who hadn't stayed in one place long in the last seven years. In his heart, he knew Tave could make him want to stay forever, but he couldn't allow that to happen. Another man was already in her life, one who could give her all the things she deserved.

He picked up his coffee cup and eased across the floor to where she stood. When he stopped beside her, she turned to him. "Thanks for bringing me your cup."

He started to set it down just as she reached for it, and their fingers touched. The contact sent his blood surging through his veins. Her eyes grew wide as if she felt the same sensation. He placed the cup in the dry sink and stared down into her eyes.

A longing like he'd never known washed over him. She stood still as his gaze moved over her face, lingered on her lips, and moved to her hair. She wore her hair down as she had the night she bent over his bed. He reached up and touched his fingertip to a curl. "Your hair is beautiful."

A nervous laugh escaped her lips. "You told me that once before."

Reason returned to him, and he let his arm drop back to his side. What was he doing? He'd never been this forward with a woman. From the moment he'd opened his eyes and seen her in that chair, he'd felt a connection to her, and his heart told him that would never change.

He took a step back from her. "I'm sorry. I shouldn't have done that."

She smiled. "That's all right, Daniel. I'm not offended."

"You should be. I'm not in the habit of being forward with engaged women."

Her forehead wrinkled. "I'm not engaged."

"Well maybe not, but you're spoken for and that's the same."

She smiled and shook her head. "I'm not spoken for, either."

"B–but your father said—"

She laughed, and the sound sent a thrill coursing through him. "I'm sure my father had a lot to say about Matthew. He doesn't really like him."

Daniel eased back to his chair and dropped into it. "Well, he did mention their differences about the war, but I encounter that with a lot of people who are very nice individuals."

She sat down across from him and leaned forward. "That's what I tell Poppa all the time, but it doesn't do any good. He also thinks Matthew flaunts his money." She planted her elbows on the table, propped her chin in her hands, and sighed. "I think it would be a blessing not to worry about money."

Daniel debated whether to ask her the question on his mind, but he wanted to know. "Are you going to marry him?"

Tave crossed her arms on the table in front of her and shrugged. "I don't know. He's going to Dauphin Island for about six weeks. He said he wants to talk to my father when he returns and that he'd like to take Poppa and me to the St. James Hotel in Selma for a few days with his family when everything's decided."

Daniel thought of the hotel on the banks of the Alabama River. "I've seen the St. James before when I was on the *Montgomery Belle*. Captain Hawkins told me that Union troops occupied it during the war. That's why it was saved."

Tave nodded. "Yes. When the city rebuilt after the war, the hotel was sold, and the new owner has redecorated it. It's quite a showplace, I've heard. My friend Savannah Rinaldi and her husband have been there. I've begged Poppa to take me, but we haven't been able to afford it. Savannah says eating in the dining room at the St. James is an experience you'll never forget."

"I've never been inside."

"Savannah says at night the dining room looks like something you might see in a palace. The tables are set with the best china, and candles glow all around the room. It even has a more elegant touch because they serve their biggest meal at night. They call it dinner, not supper like most Southerners do. She says it's the most romantic place she's ever been."

Daniel shook his head and grinned. "I would never have figured you for a romantic. You seem more like a practical woman to me."

She tossed her head and sniffed. "There are lots of things you don't know about me, Daniel Luckett."

He chuckled. "Like what?"

Tave pursed her lips and tilted her head to the side. "Well for your information, all women want romance. They want to feel like they're special. I want a man who'll show me that I'm the most important person in his life."

Tave's cheeks flushed, and she glanced down at her hands. Daniel struggled to suppress a smile. He realized she was probably telling him something she'd never shared before, and he was thrilled to be getting a glimpse into her heart. "And how will he do that?"

Her face grew redder, and she swallowed. "W–well, he'll talk to me about how he feels, and he'll ask my opinion on issues. He'll value my advice and treat me like I'm more important to him than anyone else. And even if he thinks my wishes are silly, he'll try to make them come true."

A warning flashed in his mind. His happy mood vanished at the thought of what she might want that he couldn't give her. "And just what kind of wishes do you have, Tave? To have dinner at the St. James?"

She straightened and frowned. "I suppose that's one thing I'd like to do."

Daniel's heart plummeted to the pit of his stomach. "And Matthew can afford to give you things like that."

Tave thought for a moment. "He can, but I believe there are more important things in life than what one can buy."

"Like what?"

"Like faith in God and trusting Him to lead you in the direction He wants you to go. That's the greatest wish that I have for the man I marry. I want him to trust God to lead him."

Daniel sat back in his chair and frowned. "If that's what you want, I hope you get it."

She stared at Daniel, and the intensity of her gaze caused his skin to tingle. "I don't know what I'll get, but I believe that God has a plan for me. I'm praying that God will show me what it is. He has one for you, too, Daniel. All you have to do is trust Him."

Daniel shook his head. "You sound like my mother. She used to tell me that all the time. She trusted God, but in the end He didn't do anything to help her. And I haven't seen Him doing anything to help me either."

Tave reached across the table and covered his hand with hers. "He saved your life, Daniel, and He brought two new friends into your life—my father and me. Can't you be thankful for that?"

Her soft words pricked his heart like nothing he'd heard in years. How he wished he could tell her how thankful he was he'd met her. Tears stung his eyes, and he blinked them back. "You're so much like my mother. Maybe that's why I like you."

She smiled and sat back in her chair. "I like you, too, and I'm thankful God brought you to Willow Bend. I'm just sorry it took somebody shooting you to get you off that boat."

The memory of waking to see her bending over him returned, and he knew that no matter what had brought him here, he was glad he'd come to Willow Bend. "Me, too. Now I know who's at the top of the bluff. I'll never be able to stay on board again when we dock here."

"Good. We wouldn't want to miss seeing you." She glanced over her shoulder at the dirty dishes and sighed. "Well, I'd better get those washed. Then I'm going home for the night."

He pushed back from the table and stood. "I really enjoyed my supper, Tave. You're a good cook."

"Thank you."

Daniel backed toward the door, reluctant to leave. "I think I'll go to my room. Will you be back tomorrow?"

"You can count on it. I'll be here with breakfast early in the morning. But I think my father is right. In a few days, you need to start coming to our house to eat."

"I'm looking forward to it."

Turning, he walked from the room toward his bedroom. Once inside, he shut the door and dropped into the rocking chair where Tave had sat to keep watch over him. The lamp on the table next to the chair cast a soft glow across the room. He sat back, gripped the chair arms, and closed his eyes. He rocked back and forth thinking about the conversation he'd had with Tave.

"Where were You, God?" he whispered into the quiet room. "She trusted You, and You didn't save her. And if You've been around these last seven years, You've been mighty quiet."

He opened his eyes, and his gaze fell on Tave's Bible beside the lamp. During the last week, he'd opened his eyes several times to see her reading while she sat by his bed. Now it was as if the book called his name, and he reached for it.

With trembling fingers, he caressed the leather cover. It had been years since he held a Bible. He opened the book and held it up to read the words. *"These things I have spoken unto you, that in me ye might have peace. In the world ye shall have tribulation: but be of good cheer; I have overcome the world."*

Daniel leaned his head against the back of the chair and laid the Bible in his lap. The words echoed in his mind: *"In the world ye shall have tribulation."* He'd had plenty of that. But if Jesus's words were to be believed, He could help people overcome whatever happened to them because He was always with them.

That's what Tave had been talking about, and Daniel realized she believed the promise he'd just read with all her heart. It seemed to work for her. Could it for him? He doubted it. He closed the Bible and laid it back on the table.

six

Three weeks later, Tave stepped into her father's office and knew the moment she entered that no one was there. Frowning, she stepped to the door of Daniel's room and peered inside. The patchwork quilt she'd brought from home covered the bed, and Daniel's clothes hung on the wooden pegs her father had attached to the wall when they first came to Willow Bend. Puzzled, she turned and walked back to the front door. Daniel hadn't said anything at the noon meal about going anywhere, but then he had been taking walks to get his strength back. Maybe that's where he'd gone.

She'd just stepped onto the front porch when she spied Daniel ambling down the street toward her. His rolling gait reminded her of the sailors who came ashore from time to time when their ships docked. He whistled a tune as he walked along, his hands in the pockets of his denim work pants. She recognized the tan shirt he wore, with its white collar. She'd seen it on Dante Rinaldi. No doubt Savannah had donated it to the Ladies Auxiliary at church, and it had found its way to her father's office.

Daniel's eyes lit up as he stepped on the porch. "I didn't know you were coming back this afternoon."

Tave held up the basket in her hand. "I was on my way to Mr. Perkins's store, and I thought I'd check on you first. Where have you been?"

"I've been to see Mr. Perkins. Your father told me this morning he'd talked with him about a job for me, and he wanted to meet me."

Tave frowned as she examined Daniel for any hint that he hadn't recovered enough to work. "Are you sure you're ready for this?"

"I'm feeling good. Mr. Perkins said I could start Monday." He laughed and pointed to the chairs. "Let's sit and enjoy the day for a minute." He dropped down in one of the porch chairs and wiped at his forehead. "It sure has gotten warm in the last few days."

Tave settled in the chair next to him and set her basket down. "It's the last of June, Daniel. Can you believe you've been here a month?"

"No, I can't, but I feel stronger every day."

"Well don't try to do too much in this heat. It's only going to get worse." She pulled a handkerchief from the pocket of her dress and mopped her face. "I always dread the hot weather." A breeze drifted from the river, and she smiled. "Then the river reminds me I wouldn't want to live anywhere else."

They sat in silence for a moment, and she studied him out of the corner of her eye. Color had returned to his cheeks, and he looked very different from the man who'd been brought up the riverbank to her father's office. His face didn't hold the gaunt look she'd observed on it in the days after surgery, and he was able to walk farther each day.

He turned his head toward her, and for a moment their gazes locked. Her face grew warm from the scrutiny of his eyes. A slight frown wrinkled his forehead. "What are you thinking?"

Tave struggled to control the increased beating of her heart. "I'm thankful to see you recovering so well. We really didn't expect you to live when we first saw you."

"I know." He gazed back toward the river. "I owe you and your father a lot, Tave."

She reached over and touched his arm. "You don't owe us anything, Daniel. You've given us a lot in just knowing you."

He faced her again. "How could I possibly give you anything?"

His question surprised her. Was it possible he had no idea of his worth? "You've given me so much just by being my friend. I've talked to you more in the past few weeks than I have to anyone else since I came to Willow Bend."

"You have? I would think you and your friend Savannah share all your thoughts."

"Well, she's very busy at Cottonwood, and I'm at school all the time. So we don't get to see each other much except at church."

A frown wrinkled his forehead. "I'm sure Matthew is very important to you, too."

Tave bit her lip in an attempt to keep from grinning. "Why Daniel Luckett," she said, "you remind me of Caleb Thompson, Martha's youngest son. He comes to my desk several times a day to ask if I like his brother Tad better than I do him. I wouldn't have thought a grown man could sound so much like a jealous little boy."

Daniel straightened his shoulders and took a deep breath. The muscle in his jaw twitched. "I'm only saying what is obvious. Matthew must be a mighty fine man if you're interested in him, but we don't have much in common. I've seen a lot of rich people on the *Montgomery Belle*, but they always looked at me as if I weren't really there."

Tave's heart thudded at the sadness she saw in his eyes. She'd never known anyone who put as little value on himself as Daniel did. How could she make him see his worth? She breathed a quick prayer for guidance before she spoke.

"Daniel, you are God's creature. He gave you gifts and

abilities that are yours alone. In the time I've known you, I've been struck by the fact that you are a good man who has suffered some terrible tragedies in your life. But God gave you a resourcefulness that got you through those bad times. He gave you a deep concern for other people—enough that you almost gave your life to save another's. Only a brave man would do that. I only wish I could help you with whatever happened in your past that has left deep scars on your soul."

His eyes widened. "What makes you think something happened to me?"

She'd hoped for the opportunity to broach the subject of his past ever since she first heard him cry out in his unconscious state. "I sat by your bed when you were delirious. I listened to your cries and wiped away tears that ran down your face. That first night, you were so agitated that I knelt beside you and prayed that God would calm you. I was afraid you were going to die."

He swallowed, and his Adam's apple bobbed. "I couldn't see you, but I felt you there."

"I'm glad you knew I was praying. That was the worst night. After that, I spent a lot of time on my knees beside your bed." She smiled. "And it worked. Look at you now. You're well enough to get a job."

He took a deep breath. "What did I say that concerned you so?"

"You called out for your mother. Then you yelled for someone not to hurt her."

Daniel nodded. "Yes, I suppose I did." He sat silent for a moment. "I told you that my mother married after my father's death."

"Yes."

"The man's name was Frank Jessup. He'd lost his wife

and didn't have any children. My mother thought she was doing the right thing for us. We'd have a home, and I'd have a father. It didn't take her long to realize what a mistake she'd made. Frank had a cruel streak that came out after we moved in. My mother worked from dawn till bedtime, but it was never enough for him. It only got worse when he drank. That's when the beatings began."

Pain flickered in his face, and Tave clasped her hands in her lap. "How terrible."

He glanced at her. "Yeah. It was bad. I was just a child, but I'd try to protect her. Then he'd turn on me. I didn't mind because if he was hitting me, he was letting her alone. Of course she didn't see it that way. She didn't want me hurt. I begged her over and over for us to leave, but she said we had nowhere to go. God would take care of us, she'd say. And then Frank would get drunk again."

"What happened to cause her death?"

He stared out toward the river. "I really don't know how it started. I was sixteen, and I had gone into town to get some supplies she needed. I knew he was drinking before I left, and I tried to hurry back home. When I got there, I couldn't understand why she didn't come out to meet me." A wistful smile curled his lips. "She always came running out when I'd get back from anywhere."

"But she didn't that day?"

He shook his head. "No. I had this awful feeling that something had happened. I didn't even take the horses to the barn. I just jumped out of the wagon and ran inside. She was lying on the kitchen floor. She'd been shot." He clenched his fists. "I knew he'd done it. I ran through the house looking for him. I grabbed the gun I used for hunting. The only thing on my mind was that I had to kill Frank."

Tave's heart pounded. "Did you?"

"No. He was lying in the barn with the shotgun beside him. He'd killed himself, too."

Tave wiped at a tear that rolled down her cheek. "How horrible. What did you do then?"

"I got back in the wagon and rode to my uncle's house and told him what I'd found. He went for the sheriff, and they took care of everything. The next day, we buried my mother, but I wouldn't let them bury Frank next to her. As soon as we finished, I left, and I've been drifting ever since."

"And your heart is still grieving that horrible experience."

His eyes grew wide. "Grief? For my mother, yes. I only feel hate for Frank Jessup. Sometimes I wish I'd found him before he killed himself. At least I'd have the satisfaction of knowing I avenged my mother."

Tave frowned and shook her head. "You should be thankful you didn't get a chance to kill him. You would have been executed, and for what? Vengeance? The Bible tells us that vengeance belongs to God, not to us."

"Yeah, I've heard that before, but it doesn't do anything to make me feel better." He clenched his fists at his sides. "Every time I think of Frank, it's like a knife slices through my heart and leaves me feeling like I've been cut up in little pieces and left to die."

Tave reached over and placed her hand on his arm. "I'm so sorry you've had such bad things happen in your life, Daniel. I can't even start to imagine what it's been like for you."

He stood and raked his hand through his hair. He strode to the edge of the porch, stopped, and turned to face her. "I can barely remember my father before he left for the war. But there are moments when I recall things he said and did. He was such a good man, and my mother didn't deserve to end up with Frank Jessup. If my father had lived, things would have been so different for us."

She rose and walked to where he stood. "Your father couldn't help what happened to him. Your mother did what she thought was best at the time. All you can do is lean on another Father who's waiting to help you."

He stared at her. "I've seen you reading the Bible, and I've tried that, too. I'll read something that gives me some hope I can let go of all this anger I have, and then I remember how my mother's body looked lying on that kitchen floor. I get so angry at God for letting that happen that I want to scream and ask why." He clenched his fists and glared at her. "If your God is so loving, tell me why He let that happen."

She shook her head. "People for centuries have tried to figure out why God lets bad things happen to people who love Him. My mother died when I was so young that I barely remember her, but sometimes I miss her so much that I ache inside. I used to ask my father why God took my mother away."

"What did he say?"

"He said that we aren't supposed to understand God's ways. We are just supposed to trust that He'll comfort us when bad things happen in our lives. I found a passage of scripture a long time ago that helped me cope, and I memorized it. I have to say it quite often to remind myself that God is still in control."

"What is it?"

Tave tilted her head and smiled up at Daniel. "It goes like this: 'That the trial of your faith, being much more precious than of gold that perisheth, though it be tried with fire, might be found unto praise and honour and glory at the appearing of Jesus Christ.'"

"Those sound like a lot of fancy words to me. What does it mean?"

"It reminds me that I can't control what's happening around me. Problems come, and I may be troubled for a while. But these things are necessary because they test my faith. Gold can't survive fire, but our faith is more precious than gold. If we hold on to God, we can survive. When we put our trust in God, He fills us with a peace that can endure forever. So no matter what happens in my life, God is still there, and I have to give it over to Him."

He shook his head. "You make it sound easy, but I don't know if I could ever do that."

"God has given you great trials, Daniel, but I believe He's been preparing you for something greater in your life. If you can trust Him and come out of the fire, you're going to find that God will give you the greatest peace you've ever known. And when you do that, He's going to reveal the plan He has for you."

Daniel's eyes bored into hers. "No one has ever cared enough to talk to me like you have, Tave. You almost make me feel like I'm destined for some great mission in life."

Her gaze didn't waver from his face. "Maybe you are." Then she cleared her throat, glanced around for her basket, and picked it up. "Now, I have to get to Mr. Perkins's store. You're to come to supper with Poppa tonight. Don't disappoint me."

"I won't."

Tave walked down the steps and headed toward the store. When she stopped at the store's front door, she looked back toward her father's office. Daniel still stood where she'd left him. He lifted his hand and waved.

❧

Daniel watched as Tave disappeared into the store. He turned back to the chair and sat down to ponder what he and Tave had discussed. He closed his eyes for a moment and thought about what she'd said.

For the last seven years, he'd moved from place to place in an effort to run away from the memory of what he'd seen the day he found his mother's body. Hatred had burned in his heart for the man who'd destroyed the last person Daniel had in his life, and he didn't know if he could ever let go of the past.

Tave's words returned to him, and he remembered how she looked when she gazed at him. In her eyes, he saw genuine concern for him. She wanted his soul to be at peace, and her words almost persuaded him he could be. His feelings for her made him want to do what she asked, but something still held him back.

When he'd first seen Tave, an emotion he hadn't experienced in years had grabbed his heart. Over the past few weeks as he'd gotten to know her, it had only deepened. There was no doubt about it. He was in love with her. It didn't matter, though. He could never speak of it. He wasn't the kind of man she'd described as the husband she wanted. She deserved so much more than a penniless wanderer haunted by a memory that controlled his life.

He'd never had trouble leaving any other place behind, and when the time came, he'd leave Tave, too. She needed someone like Matthew Chandler, a man with money and family connections. He could make all her wishes come true.

A discreet cough at the edge of the porch caught his attention, and he glanced up to see Martha Thompson standing there. He'd spoken with her several times when she'd brought food to the doctor's office for them.

He had discovered as soon as he met her that she knew everything about all the residents of Willow Bend. He wondered what gossip she was pedaling today. Stifling an inward groan, he stood and smiled. "Mrs. Thompson, imagine seeing you today."

She grinned at him. "I was just on my way back from the store, and I saw you sittin' out here all alone. I thought I'd check on you and see how you're doing."

"I'm fine. And you?"

"Just tolerable, Mr. Luckett. Just tolerable." She frowned and twisted her shoulders. "Been havin' some trouble with my back lately. Walking back and forth to town sure does cause my rheumatism to act up."

His hope that this was going to be a quick greeting vanished. He pointed to the chair where Tave had sat. "Would you like to rest for a while?"

Martha shook her head. "I don't want to bother you none."

Guilt at wishing he'd slipped inside Dr. Spencer's office before Martha saw him niggled at the back of his mind. After all, she had fed him while he was sick. "How could you bother me? Especially after all the good food you've fed me."

She giggled. "Now ain't you a smooth talker? I was just doing my Christian duty to help out folks in need."

"And I appreciate it."

She eased up onto the porch and plopped down in one of the chairs. She exhaled and set the basket beside her. "It sure is a hot day. I reckon I could stand to sit a spell before I take that long walk back home." She glanced at him. "Mr. Perkins tells me you gonna start working for him next week."

Daniel nodded and dropped into the chair next to her. "I am. I need to earn some money so I can get on up to Montgomery."

She tilted her head to one side. "You got family up that way?"

"No. My family's all dead.

"You don't have a wife?"

"I'm afraid not."

"Then what's in Montgomery?"

"I have a job waiting for me there."

"Doin' what?"

"Working on the docks."

The questions had been fired at him with the rapid precision of a Gatling gun. It took Daniel only a minute to figure out that Martha had accomplished her mission. She'd found out what she wanted to know about him.

Martha narrowed her eyes and nodded. "You don't say. On the docks, huh? I know Doc and Tave are gonna miss you. They appear to be quite taken with you."

"I am with them, too. After all, they saved my life."

Martha shifted in her chair and gazed at him, starting at his toes and ending at his head. "You sure look different than you did that day they brought you up that bluff. Me and the other ladies thought you was a goner for sure. Now that you're feeling better, all of us in the Ladies Auxiliary hope you'll come to church."

"Dr. Spencer mentioned to me how kind all of you were by bringing clothes for me and of course the food you brought. I'd love to meet everyone."

Martha's face lit up. "Now that'd just be wonderful. I want to make sure you meet my daughter Esther. She cooked a lot of that food I brought over here, and she's just dying to meet you."

Daniel gulped and forced a smile to his face. "I'll be happy to meet Esther and thank her."

Martha pushed to her feet, placed her hands in the small of her back, and rubbed. "That little rest helped a lot." She bent down and picked up her basket. "I guess I can make it home now. Maybe we'll see you Sunday."

"Maybe so."

He watched Martha as she waddled down the street, then turned his attention back to Mr. Perkins's store. Tave stepped onto the street, a blond woman behind her. They chatted as they strolled down the street toward Dr. Spencer's office.

When they reached it, they stepped onto the porch, and Tave pointed to the woman with her. "Daniel, this is my friend Savannah Rinaldi. She and her husband own Cottonwood Plantation."

Daniel had heard Tave and her father talk about the Rinaldis before, but he hadn't had the opportunity to meet either of them. "Captain Hawkins pointed out your home to me once when we passed going upriver. He told me you and your husband rebuilt the house to what it was like before it burned."

Savannah smiled. "Well, almost to what it was like. It's somewhat smaller, but we like it fine. I'm sorry my husband isn't with me today. I know he'd like to meet you." Her eyes lit up as if she'd just been struck with an idea. "Tave, why don't you bring Daniel to the picnic after church on Sunday?"

A shy smile pulled at Tave's lips, and she tightened her grip on the basket's handle. "I was going to ask you if you felt up to doing that. What do you think?"

He hadn't wanted to go to church in years, but he wanted to be wherever Tave was. If that meant going to church, he'd do it. His plans might call for him to leave Willow Bend, but until he did, he intended to spend every minute he could with her.

"I'd love to go."

seven

Tave and Savannah walked toward the livery stable that sat at the end of the main street. Tave walked past there often on her way back and forth to her father's office and always stopped to look at the horses in the corral at the side of the building. As she and Savannah approached the fence, a chestnut mare with a white star on her head trotted over and whinnied at them.

Tave stopped and stared at the beautiful creature. The mare stuck her head over the fence, and Tave patted her. "Where did you come from, girl? I haven't seen you before."

Savannah stepped up beside Tave. "Dante said Mr. Jensen bought some new horses at the sale in Selma last week. She must be one of them."

Tave took in the sleek lines of the mare. "Whoever gets her is going to be a lucky person." She gave the horse one last pat, and she and Savannah walked on toward the front of the livery stable. Tave darted a glance at her friend. "I'm glad you invited Daniel to church. I wanted to, but I wasn't sure he'd come."

Savannah stopped and stared at her. "Why would you think that?"

Tave longed to discuss her conversation with Daniel, but she didn't want to reveal anything about his background that he wanted to keep private. "Daniel has had some problems in his past, and I've tried to give him some scriptures to help him. I thought he might think I was pushing him too much.

It was much better coming from you."

"I don't think you'd have a problem getting him to do anything you wanted."

"Why do you say that?"

Savannah laughed and stared at Tave with a look of disbelief. "What's the matter with you? Are you blind?"

Tave's mouth gaped open. "Blind about what?"

Savannah pursed her lips and studied Tave. "You can't see that he's in love with you, can you?"

Tave pressed her hand to her chest and took a step back. "In love with me? What makes you think that?"

"It's the way he looks at you, Tave. I can see it in his eyes."

Tave could hardly believe what she was hearing. She knew Daniel had developed an attachment to her. But love? No, that couldn't be. Tave shook her head. "You're wrong. I'd know it if that were true."

Savannah looped her arm through Tave's, and they moved toward Savannah's buggy that sat outside the livery stable. "Not necessarily. I remember Mamie telling me that Dante loved me, and I didn't believe it. Later, I didn't know how I'd missed all the signals he'd been sending me."

Tave's stomach churned, and her knees felt weak. "B—but what should I do?"

Savannah stopped at her buggy and placed her basket inside. "Nothing, I suppose. That is, unless you want to encourage him." Savannah turned to face Tave, and her eyes grew wide. "You're in love with him, too, aren't you?"

The question stunned Tave. She reached out and clutched the side of the buggy for support. "I—I don't know. I like him, and I feel very protective of him. I thought that was because I'd taken care of him when he was so sick."

Savannah nodded in the direction of the livery stable. "I

need to go pay Mr. Jensen what I owe him. You get in the buggy, and I'll take you home. I think we need to talk about this more."

Tave climbed in and settled on the seat. Savannah's words whirled in her mind as she waited for her friend to return. Was it possible Daniel was in love with her? And what about her feelings? She put her fingers on her temples and rubbed. This was too much to comprehend.

Savannah returned in a few minutes and untied the reins from the hitching post. When she was settled in the buggy, she turned the horse in the direction of Tave's house.

They rode in silence for a minute until Tave's curiosity got the best of her. She turned to Savannah. "How did you know when you fell in love with Dante?"

Savannah arched her eyebrows and flicked the reins across the horse's back. "It's hard to put into words. I think it began with respect. I saw what a good man he was even though he'd had some bad things happen to him in the past. I recognized his strength of character because he was able to survive some terrible experiences, but it hadn't hardened his heart."

Tave nodded. "Daniel's had some horrible things happen to him. He hasn't been able to put some of it behind him yet. I don't know if he ever will." She glanced at Savannah. "He's carrying a lot of anger inside him, but I know he's a good man. He risked his life to save another man's life. Someone who does that has to be brave. Captain Hawkins said he's a fine young man, too."

"Then you can be assured he is. I've known Captain Hawkins since I was a child, and he's a good judge of character. But Tave, you know as well as I do that there are many people who look good in the eyes of the world, but they don't have a personal relationship with Jesus." They rode in silence for a while before

Savannah spoke again. "What about Matthew? How do you feel about him?"

With a start, Tave realized she'd hardly thought about Matthew since he'd been away. She bit down on her lip, then glanced at Savannah. "I haven't told you what Matthew said before he left with his mother."

When she finished telling Savannah of Matthew's visit, Savannah shook her head. "He talked about marriage, but he never said he loved you?"

Tave gasped. "You're right. I just now realized that."

Savannah grabbed the reins with one hand and reached over to pat Tave's arm. "I'm sure he must, or he wouldn't want to marry you."

Tave nodded, but she wasn't so sure. The first time she'd seen Matthew after coming to Willow Bend she had thought him the most handsome man she'd ever seen, but he'd never noticed her until a year ago. Since that time, she'd often dreamed of what it would be like to be married to the heir of one of the biggest plantations in Alabama. Now she realized she'd ceased having those thoughts some time ago, and she hadn't questioned why.

Why would Matthew talk of marrying her if he didn't love her? And what about Daniel? Was it possible he'd fallen in love with her?

Tave clenched her fists and pounded her knees. "Why is it so hard sometimes to know what God's will is for your life?"

Savannah laughed. "I've often wondered that myself." She pulled the horse to a stop at Tave's house and turned in the seat to face her. "The important thing is for you to pray about it, and search your heart for the answer, Tave. Matthew has a lot of money, but it doesn't mean a thing if you don't love him. On the other hand, Daniel seems like a nice enough young man, but he doesn't recognize the need for God in his life. Be careful. He could end up hurting you. You're my friend, and I don't want to see that happen."

Tave hugged Savannah and smiled. "Thank you. I'll think about everything you've said, and I'll pray about it. For all I know, there may be somebody else God has in mind for me. I'll wait until the Lord reveals what He has planned for me."

"That sounds good to me. We'll talk again. Maybe we'll have a chance to do that Sunday at the picnic."

Tave climbed from the buggy and waved as the horse trotted down the street. When her friend was out of sight, she walked toward the small house where she and her father had lived since coming to Willow Bend.

She stopped at the crepe myrtle bush outside the front door and broke off several branches to arrange in the cut-glass vase that had belonged to her grandmother. The deep pink blooms always added a festive touch to their dining table, and she wanted everything to look special for Daniel tonight.

Her heart quickened at the memory of Savannah's words. Did Daniel love her? She had to admit she harbored special feelings for him, but she hadn't called it love. Not yet, anyway.

❧

On Saturday night, Tave closed the cupboard and turned back to survey the clean kitchen. Every supper dish had been washed, dried, and put away. A burst of laughter came from the parlor, and she smiled. She knew that sound all too well. Poppa had just defeated Daniel in another game of checkers.

She picked up the oil lamp from the kitchen table and walked into the parlor. Daniel gazed down at the checkerboard as if trying to determine which move had proved his undoing in the match. Her father leaned back in his chair, crossed his legs, and tapped his tented fingers together. A smile curled his lips.

Tave set the lamp down on the table next to the rocker that had belonged to her mother and sat down. She plumped a pillow behind her back and sighed. "Don't bother trying to recall the moves, Daniel. I'm sure if you ask Poppa, he can tell you where you made your mistake."

Daniel looked up, a puzzled expression on his face. "How do you know that?"

"Because I've been watching him defeat every guest we've had ever since I can remember. It's an obsession with him. Behind that kind face and loving personality lurks a fierce competitor who shows no mercy."

Her father laughed and pushed to his feet. "You're speaking ill of your father, my dear. I would expect better from my daughter."

The bag that held items to be darned sat on the floor at her feet, and she reached for it. "You forget how well I know you, Poppa." She pulled a sock from inside and cast a glance at Daniel. "I learned a long time ago that checkers is a scientific game, and Poppa plays it well. He's not so concerned about his own moves as he is about waiting for the right moment when his opponent makes a mistake. Then he strikes swiftly."

Daniel rose and stuck his hands in his pockets. "Well, I have to say playing with him these past few weeks has been quite a learning experience."

Her father slapped Daniel on the back. "Keep practicing, son. Who knows? You just might be the one to beat me."

Daniel shook his head. "I doubt that, but I enjoyed the game."

Her father stifled a yawn. "Now if you two will excuse

me, I have some work to do. I have a sick patient out at Winterville Plantation, the son of one of the tenant farmers, and I need to do some research about his condition. I'm going to my bedroom and see what I can find in that new medical book that came the other day."

Tave smiled at him. "Don't nod off to sleep in your chair and forget to blow out the lamp."

"I'll be careful."

She watched as her father walked from the room and entered his bedroom before she glanced back at Daniel, who stared at her. He jerked his gaze away from her face and turned back to the chair where he'd sat.

They sat in silence as she began to mend her father's sock. After a time, Daniel stood and walked over to the mantel. He picked up a daguerreotype and stared at it. He glanced over his shoulder at her. "Your mother?"

She nodded. "Yes, it was made while my parents were on their wedding trip to New York. Poppa's often told me how excited she was that day and how she fussed with her hair. She had trouble picking out which of the embossed leather cases she wanted. She told my father she hoped the likeness would show him how happy she was to be his wife. It's the only picture I have of her, and of course it's my father's greatest treasure."

"She was very beautiful."

"Thank you, Daniel, for saying that." She rose, crossed the room to stand beside him at the mantel, and gazed at the picture of her mother. "That's her wedding dress. I still have it. It's a cream-colored silk-satin dress. My grandmother hand sewed the appliquéd lace you see on the skirt and at the end of the sleeves. Poppa says she looked like a queen when she walked into the church."

Daniel replaced the shiny image to the mantel and turned to Tave. "You look just like her, you know."

Tave shook her head. "No, she was much prettier than I am."

He glanced at the likeness one more time. "Your hair is the same, and so is your smile. I think you're wrong about this picture being your father's greatest treasure."

"Why?"

He took a deep breath. "I think *you* are his greatest treasure because he sees her in you every day."

Tave started to protest, but she remembered how she would often catch her father staring at her, tears in his eyes. He would look away quickly. She wondered if he might be thinking of her mother and the happy times they shared. She turned to face him. "I do look like her, don't I?"

He trailed his fingertips down the side of her cheek. "You're the most beautiful woman I've ever seen in my life. I wish I could tell you. . ."

Tave frowned at Daniel's hesitation. "Tell me what?"

He pulled his hand away from her face and let his arm fall to his side. His eyes that had ignited her heart with the fire she saw in them a few moments before looked as if they were blocks of ice. He backed away from her.

"How much I enjoyed my supper. Now I think I'd better go."

Tave frowned and took a step toward him, but he turned and headed for the front door. It only took her a moment before she reacted. She rushed across the floor and stepped in front of him, blocking his exit from the room. "I think you were going to tell me something else. What is it?"

He licked his lips. "I—I was going to say. . ." He gritted his teeth and raked his hand through his hair. He exhaled and shook his head. "It was nothing important, Tave."

His hand trembled, and she touched his arm. "Daniel,

please, if it's something I can help you with. . ."

His eyes grew wide, and he jerked away from her. "It's nothing for you to be concerned about." He pushed past her. "Now I need to leave. I'll be here in the morning to go to church with you and your father. Have a good night."

He'd hardly finished saying the words before the door slammed behind him. Tave stood in the parlor unsure what had just occurred. One minute, Daniel had reached out to her in a way that could only mean he had some feelings for her. Then he'd shattered the mood with his hasty departure.

She had the impression that his leaving so abruptly meant he wanted to distance himself from her in more ways than one. The reality of what she'd tried to deny hit her. The feelings she had for Daniel weren't caused by how she'd taken care of him when he was near death. What she felt could only mean one thing: She had come to love Daniel Luckett.

eight

Daniel leaned against the hitching post outside the Spencer home, closed his eyes, and lifted his face to the warm Sunday morning sun. He wondered if Tave would be glad to see him after the way he'd rushed out of the house last night. He had to leave, though, because he was on the verge of making a terrible mistake.

When he'd seen how much she looked like the beautiful woman in the picture, he'd been overcome with a longing to let her know how much she'd come to mean to him. Now in the light of day, he thought he'd put that moment of weakness behind him. He wouldn't think of her that way anymore. From now on, he would think of her as a dear friend, one he was going to attend church with today.

He chuckled at the thought of him in church. If someone had told him two months ago he'd be excited about attending church, he would have denied it. But now that he was about to do it, he knew it was time. He longed to put the past behind him, but every time it almost seemed possible, Frank Jessup's face would flash in his memory. Then the hatred would overflow again.

He'd spent hours reading Tave's Bible in the past few weeks. The scriptures she'd given him, as well as others he'd found on his own, had spoken to his heart. One he'd read last night still lingered in his mind: *"If ye continue in my word, then are ye my disciples indeed; And ye shall know the truth, and the truth shall make you free."*

That's what he needed—to be free of the past.

A creaking sound caught his attention, and he straightened to see Dr. Spencer leading his horse, hitched to a buggy, around the side of the house. Daniel had watched Dr. Spencer leave in the buggy to visit a sick person many times since he'd been staying at his office. Nothing kept the dedicated doctor from going where he was needed. Just last week, he'd watched Dr. Spencer huddle under the buggy's top as he guided his horse out of town in the midst of a driving rainstorm.

This morning, the overhead covering of the buggy lay folded to the rear of the backseat. Dr. Spencer raised a hand in greeting as he approached. "Morning, Daniel. You didn't have to walk over here. I would have stopped to get you at the office."

Daniel inhaled. "I know, but it's such a nice day I wanted to walk."

"It's good to see you've recovered enough that you can walk."

Daniel grinned and thumped his chest. "I've got my strength back just in time to begin my new job tomorrow."

Dr. Spencer looped the horse's reins over the hitching post and walked around to pat the horse's flank. "Ah yes. You're going to start helping Mr. Perkins tomorrow, but be careful. I don't want you overdoing it."

"I will be."

Dr. Spencer pulled out his pocket watch, glanced at the time, and frowned. "Where is that girl? We're going to be late if she doesn't hurry." He cupped his hands around his mouth. "Tave! Aren't you ready yet?"

The front door of the house opened, and Tave stepped onto the porch. She held a basket in one hand as she reached back to close the door. "I'm coming, Poppa."

Dr. Spencer's eyebrows arched, and he sighed. "Daniel, there's something about women you need to find out while you're still single. They're never ready on time. They'll keep a man waiting just to see him squirm."

Tave laughed and glided down the flagstone walkway toward them. "Don't believe a word of what he says, Daniel." She arched an eyebrow. "That is, if you expect to get any of my fried chicken at the picnic today."

Her father laughed, took the basket, and set it in the backseat. "Maybe I'd better rephrase my observation about women, Daniel. The appearance of a beautiful woman can always make you forget your annoyance over her being late." His eyes twinkled. "Especially when she arrives with fried chicken."

Daniel heard the exchange between the two, but his tongue felt glued to the roof of his mouth. All he could do was gape at Tave like a schoolboy. He'd never seen her more beautiful than she was today. The lavender and white dress she wore had rows of ruffles draped down the skirt-back, and it swished with every step she took. Her auburn hair pinned on top of her head sparkled in the sun. As she brushed past him, the scent of lilacs filled his nostrils.

As if she could read his thoughts, she lowered her eyelids and smiled. "I'm glad you wanted to come today, Daniel. You'll get to meet all our friends. I hope Dante gets to come with Savannah and the children. I think you'd really like him."

"I hope so, too. I enjoyed meeting Savannah."

She lifted the hem of her dress with one hand to climb into the buggy, and he grasped her other arm to assist. His skin burned from the touch. He bit down on his lip in an effort to keep from revealing the emotions whirling through him.

Once she was seated, she spread her full skirt out and glanced at him. "Thank you, Daniel."

He mumbled something, he had no idea what, and climbed in behind them. He settled against the leather backseat of the buggy and watched Dr. Spencer turn the horse and guide it along the road toward the Willow Bend Church. The gentle pressure the doctor used to prod the animal gave evidence of how well the horse and handler understood each other, a knowledge that had most likely been acquired by spending untold hours traveling from farm to farm around Willow Bend.

Dr. Spencer chuckled and glanced over his shoulder. "You might as well get ready, Daniel. I expect you're going to be swamped with mothers trying to introduce their unmarried daughters to you. It's not often we get eligible bachelors in Willow Bend, and you've been the topic of conversation ever since you got here."

Daniel's face grew warm, and he squinted up at the sun. "Aw, they won't care about a man like me."

"What does that mean?"

"Just that I'm a drifter, never have settled down anywhere. As soon as I feel like it, I guess I'll be moving on."

His stomach churned at the words he'd spoken. It was true he'd never been interested in settling in one spot before, not until he met Tave, but that didn't do him any good. A woman like her needed someone who could give her a better life than he could.

Dr. Spencer nodded. "Well that's up to you, but we'd like to see you stay around if you'd like to."

"Thanks, Dr. Spencer."

Daniel stared at Tave to see how his words had affected her, but she didn't move or speak. Her rigid back seemed to convey the message that she didn't care whether he stayed or left. With a sigh, he directed his attention back to the road ahead.

The church that Dr. Spencer told him had been built in the early part of the century came into view. Buggies and some farm wagons dotted the area around the front of the building, which sat well back from the road leading out of town. On one side of the church, tombstones marked the graves of past worshippers, and a stand of water oaks fanned across the field on the opposite side. Tables had been set underneath the trees in preparation for the picnic that would follow services.

Daniel hopped from the buggy and helped Tave down. Without looking at him, she held out her hand and grasped his. Once on the ground, she pointed to the basket. "We'll take that inside. I don't want it to sit outside in the heat."

He nodded and reached for the basket. Dr. Spencer walked around the front of the buggy from where he'd tied the horse and put his hands in his pockets. "Well, are you ready to meet all the good folks of Willow Bend, Daniel?"

His stomach churned, and Daniel glanced down at his clothes. Even though they were the best he had, he supposed everybody would be better dressed today than he was. He swallowed and looked up at Dr. Spencer. "Am I dressed all right?"

For the first time, Tave looked at him and smiled. "We don't judge a man by how he's dressed, Daniel." She studied him with a critical gaze before she nodded as if satisfied. "You look very handsome. Now why don't you escort me inside? I'm sure Martha Thompson would love something to talk about tomorrow at Mr. Perkins's store."

He stared down at her small hand resting on his arm, and

he thought his heart would burst with love. At that moment, he didn't want to be anywhere else besides right here with Tave. He straightened to his full height and crooked his arm. "I'd consider myself the luckiest man in the world to take you into church."

She looped her arm through his and moved closer to him. "Then let's go hear what message Reverend Somers has for us today."

Daniel's feet felt like they barely touched the ground as they walked to the church and entered. Once inside, Tave pointed to a small room at the side of the entrance where other baskets sat, and he deposited hers inside before they joined the already-gathered congregation.

During the walk down the aisle and as they stepped into a pew near the front, Daniel felt all eyes staring at him. He sat down between Tave and Dr. Spencer and jumped when someone tapped him on the shoulder. He turned to see Savannah Rinaldi behind him. "I want to introduce you to my husband. Dante, this is Daniel Luckett, the young man who saved Captain Hawkins's life."

A broad-shouldered, dark-complexioned man leaned forward, his hand outstretched. "Glad to meet you, Daniel. Captain Hawkins is a friend of our family. Thank you for what you did."

Daniel stared into the darkest eyes he thought he'd ever seen. He grasped Dante's hand. "Anybody else would have done the same."

Dante shook his head. "I doubt that." Dante glanced toward the front of the church where Reverend Somers was about to take his place at the pulpit and whispered to Daniel. "There's something we need to talk about, but we'll do that later at the picnic. Glad to have you here today."

Daniel's body tensed. What could this man he'd only just met have to talk about with him? With a nod in Dante's direction, Daniel swiveled in the pew to face forward.

Next to him, Tave leaned close and whispered in his ear. "I'm glad you've already made a friend."

He started to reply that this new friend had said something that puzzled him, but Reverend Somers's voice rang out. "Let's begin our service today by standing and repeating the Lord's Prayer together."

Daniel rose to his feet with the rest of the congregation and gazed at the small wooden cross on the table in front of the pulpit. An open Bible lay beside it. Peace flowed through him at the sight. He hadn't been in a church since his mother had taken him when he was a child, but it felt natural to be here.

He bowed his head and closed his eyes. He didn't move as the familiar words spoken by the congregation washed over him. "Our Father, who art in heaven, hallowed be thy name. . . ."

❧

Daniel could hardly believe all the food the ladies of the church had brought, and each one insisted he have some of hers. He'd felt like the guest of honor at a big celebration ever since they'd left the church for the picnic grove.

He finally escaped all the attention when Tave and Savannah rescued him and led him toward a towering oak tree where they had spread a quilt on the ground. Dante already sat there, his plate piled high with enough food to feed two men. He grinned and motioned Daniel to sit beside him.

❧

Now with his plate empty, Dante set it aside and rubbed his stomach. "I don't think I'll be able to eat another bite for a week after that good meal."

Savannah arched her eyebrows and tilted her head to the side. "Is that so? Then I assume that means I won't have to fix you any supper."

He grinned, leaned over, and planted a kiss on his wife's cheek. "I wouldn't want to deny you the pleasure of cooking for your devoted husband."

She swatted at his arm and glanced at Tave. "Do you see what I have to deal with? He's a charmer, and I'm helpless to resist him."

Tave nodded. "I see what you mean."

Daniel watched the couple stare into each other's eyes like there was no one else around. Their feelings for each other were evident for everyone to see, and he thought how fortunate they were to love like that. He glanced at Tave and saw her studying him. She dropped her gaze and reached for the dirty dishes.

"We'd better get this cleaned up before Martha comes around to find out what's taking us so long."

Savannah pushed to her feet, and Dante handed her their dishes. She smiled down at her husband. "While we're gone, I think you have something to talk to Daniel about."

"I do."

Daniel watched Tave and Savannah walk across the picnic area to the table where the ladies were in the process of putting food away and gathering up dirty dishes before he turned back to Dante. "You said something in church about wanting to talk with me. What is it?"

Dante pushed to his feet. "Do you mind if we walk and talk? I've been sitting about as long as I can stand it."

"Fine with me. I was about to get stiff from sitting on the ground."

They walked toward the front of the church and stopped at the edge of the small cemetery. Dante pointed to a grave. "That's Savannah's aunt. I only met her a few weeks before her death, but she was a great lady."

Daniel nodded. "She must have had a big influence on Savannah. She's one of the nicest women I've ever met."

Dante grinned. "Nicer than Tave?"

Daniel almost choked on the surprise that clogged his throat. "Wh—what?"

Dante slapped him on the back and grinned. "Sorry. I couldn't resist. It's plain to see how you feel about Tave, but that's not what I wanted to talk to you about."

"Then what is it?"

He stared back at the grave. "Savannah's Aunt Jane was a good friend of Captain Hawkins. When she needed money so badly, he bought her house with the understanding that she could live there until her death. He felt by that time he'd be ready to retire to Willow Bend, and he would take over the house then."

"But he never has."

Dante nodded. "That's right. Aunt Jane died seven years ago, but Captain Hawkins can't leave the river. He will someday, but not yet." Dante motioned for Daniel to follow him, and they strolled toward the back of the church. "Anyway, when Captain Hawkins came ashore to see you a few weeks ago, he left a letter at Mr. Perkins's store for me. I had to take care of something before I could tell you what the letter said."

Daniel stopped and stared at Dante. "Was it about me?"

"Yes. He's very thankful to you for saving his life. Since he's not going to be coming back for a few months, he wanted to do something to help you."

Daniel held up his hands in protest. "He doesn't owe me

anything. He always treated me like I was somebody when I worked for him. He wasn't like other men I've known."

Dante's dark eyes narrowed. "Captain Hawkins treated you like you were somebody because you are. He knows, as I do, that you're a child of God, and because of that, you have great value."

A nervous laugh escaped Daniel's mouth. "That's what Tave says."

"Well, she's right. Anyway, Captain Hawkins was worried that you might lose your job in Montgomery if you stayed here too long. He talked to the man who hired you there and told him what had happened. So they're holding your job for a while, but it won't be there if you wait too long."

"There's nothing I can do about that right now. I don't have the money to get to Montgomery. I could walk, but I'm not sure I'm strong enough for that yet."

Dante nodded. "That's what Captain Hawkins thought. So he left me enough money to buy you a horse and saddle and to pay for the horse's upkeep until you decide to leave. Mr. Jensen at the livery stable found me one last week, and he's taking care of it for now."

Daniel gasped. "Captain Hawkins bought me a horse?"

Dante chuckled. "Yes. She's a pretty thing. Chestnut with a white star on her forehead, and gentle. I think you're going to like her." Dante reached into his pocket and took out a piece of folded paper. "And there's money left over for you to have. This is to help you get on your feet."

With trembling fingers, Daniel unfolded the paper and stared at the money inside. He'd never seen so much in his life. He struggled to speak, but he was afraid he was going to cry instead. "Th–th–this is too much. Did Captain Hawkins leave all this?"

Dante glanced down to the ground and kicked at a tuft of grass. "Well, Dr. Spencer and I helped out a little bit, too."

Daniel folded the paper back and frowned. "I don't understand. Why would you do something for me? You don't even know me."

Dante stared past Daniel as if he were remembering something. "When I was young, Daniel, there was a time when I was alone in the world. Just like you. A kind man in Mobile helped me, and because of him, great things happened in my life. This gift we're giving you is to let you know that there are better things waiting for you, too. You just have to let God lead you to where they are." He pointed to the money in Daniel's hand. "Someday you're going to come across somebody who needs help. When that happens, remember your friends who helped you."

Daniel had never known people like those he'd met from Willow Bend. There was something in their lives that was different from what he'd seen in the lives of other people he'd met in his travels. He clutched the money and tried to control his trembling lips. "Thank you, Dante. It's been a long time since I've met anyone like all the friends I've made in Willow Bend. I appreciate everything you and Captain Hawkins have done for me. And of course, I wouldn't even be here if it wasn't for Dr. Spencer and Tave."

Dante laughed. "Speaking of Tave, I think we'd better get back to the ladies before they come searching for us."

They ambled back to the picnic grove, and Daniel spied Tave and Savannah coming toward them. His pulse quickened as it did every time he saw Tave. She smiled, and something told him it was for him alone.

He thought of the people who were making changes in his life—Captain Hawkins, Dr. Spencer, Dante Rinaldi, but most of all Tave. He didn't want to think about Matthew Chandler and how she might feel about him. At the moment, all he knew was that he loved her. If God really wanted to help him, then maybe Tave wasn't unattainable to him after all.

nine

With the meal over, the congregation drifted into small groups across the picnic area. Women clustered in the shade of the trees and fanned themselves as the afternoon grew warmer. The men stood in groups discussing the weather and its possible effects on the crops.

Tave and Daniel drifted from group to group, stopping long enough for Daniel to be introduced to those he hadn't met. Tave glanced at him out of the corner of her eye as Martha Thompson waddled toward them, her daughter Esther following behind.

Martha waved in greeting. "Daniel. Come here and meet my daughter Esther. I told you 'bout her. Remember?"

Daniel stopped in front of Martha and smiled. "Of course I do." He nodded in Esther's direction. "I understand I have you to thank for some of that good food I ate while I was recuperating."

Esther looked down at the ground and dug the toe of her shoe in the dirt. "Yeah. Me and Ma was glad to help out."

Daniel thumped his chest. "Well, it worked. I'm back to good health."

Martha nudged her daughter. "Didn't I tell you he was a smooth talker?" She turned back to Daniel. "What you gonna do now that you're well? Still going to Montgomery?"

Tave's heart raced when he cast a quick glance in her direction. "I'm not sure when that will be," he said.

Martha pulled her daughter closer. "Well, don't you go off

without visiting us sometime. You hear?"

"I won't."

Daniel glanced at her, and Tave almost giggled at the silent plea in his eyes for her to help him. She stepped forward. "It's good to see you and Esther today, Martha. Now if you'll excuse us, I want to introduce Daniel to some more of our friends."

She took Daniel's arm and pulled him toward a group that sat near one of the tables. Before they reached them, a whoop sounded from nearby, and the girls from her school ran toward them and surrounded Tave.

"Miss Spencer," Sarah Jensen said, "we want you to come play hopscotch with us."

Tave laughed. "You're not serious."

Katie Tyler nodded. "Yes, we are. All year at school you said you'd play one day, but you never did. Now we want you to do it."

Tave shook her head and tried to back away from the girls surrounding her. "I haven't played hopscotch since I was a child."

Gabby Rinaldi looked up at her with a mischievous grin. A gap where the six-year-old had lost a tooth a few days before flashed behind her smile. "You can do it, Miss Spencer."

"Please, please." The chorus of voices rose on the afternoon air.

Some of the boys who were chasing one another across the far end of the picnic area stopped and stared in the direction of the girls' voices. One of them whistled and pointed to Tave. With a shout, they ran forward and converged at the spot where the girls circled Tave.

"You gonna play hopscotch, Miss Spencer?" Tad Thompson shouted.

Hoping for an ally, Tave cast a glance at Daniel. "Aren't you going to help me?"

He spread his hands in resignation. "Far be it from me to go up against a group of determined children."

Tave smiled as her gaze drifted over the children she'd taught for the past year at the Willow Bend School. Bending over, she reached out and cupped Gabby's chin in her hand. "All right, I'll play. But if I fall, somebody had better catch me."

A shout went up from the group. "We will. We will."

Tave glanced at Daniel who ambled along behind the group leading her to the hopscotch course. "A fine friend you turned out to be."

Daniel stuck his hands in his pockets and grinned. "I'm enjoying this. Just like you seemed to enjoy my visit with Martha and Esther."

She glared at him. "Traitor."

Gabby eased up beside Tave and slipped a smooth, flat stone in her hand. "Use this one, Miss Spencer. It's my lucky marker."

They reached the hopscotch course, and the children fanned out around it. Silence descended over the group. Tave glanced over at Daniel, who had walked to a nearby tree and leaned against it. He gave her a small salute, and she frowned at him.

Stepping to the first square, Tave gazed at the slightly crooked lines of the course that two of the older girls had scratched into the black dirt with a sharp stone. Three single squares lay one on top of another with two lateral squares atop them. Another single square with a double square on top of it completed the course. Stones lay in the first square.

"Hey, Miss Spencer, you know you can't jump in the squares that have markers, don't you?" Tad giggled and punched

Johnny Williams in the ribs. Laughter rippled through the assembled group.

Tave arched an eyebrow and stared at him. "I know, Tad."

A hush fell over the children as Tave bent forward at the waist and lobbed her stone to the second square. A puff of dust drifted upward as it plopped to the ground.

Tave took a deep breath, balanced on one foot, and began her journey by easily hopping over the first two squares. She reached the end and planted both feet in the two squares there, whirled around, and hopped on one foot back toward the beginning.

When she entered the third box, she stopped and held one arm out to balance herself. With deliberate movements she bent toward the stone resting in the second square, clasped it in her fingers, and looked up with a victory smile. The minute she did she realized her mistake. Her body swayed, and she struggled to keep from falling. It was no use.

A high-pitched squeal pierced the air as the children scurried back. Tave toppled forward and landed facedown in the dirt, her arms spread out to the side. No one moved. Then a dozen hands pulled at her until she pushed herself up into a sitting position. The girls knelt in a circle around her, and the boys hovered behind.

"Miss Spencer, are you all right?" Their voices all seemed to speak at once.

Dust covered the front of the lavender and white dress she'd worn in an attempt to impress Daniel. She blew at a strand of hair that hung in her eye and let her gaze drift over twenty worried faces. "I thought I told you to catch me."

Gabby dropped to her knees. "I tried, Miss Spencer, but Tad got in my way."

Tave brushed the dirt from the front of her dress and

started to get to her feet. A strong hand gripped her arm, and she stared up into the twinkling blue eyes of Daniel. "Allow me." He bit down on his lip, but he couldn't suppress the laughter shaking his body.

She allowed him to pull her up. When she'd regained her balance, she brushed her hair out of her eyes. Unable to help herself, she smiled down at the children clustered around them. "Well, it looks like I'm going to have to practice if I'm going to win at hopscotch." She bent over and chucked Gabby under the chin. "I tell you what. When school starts, I'm going to challenge all of the girls to a contest. Then we'll see who the hopscotch champion of Willow Bend School is."

The children's cheers echoed across the picnic grounds. Several adults glanced in their direction, smiled, and turned back to their conversations.

"Come on. Let's go play," Tad cried, and the boys raced after each other toward the tree line at the back of the picnic area.

Daniel pulled a clean handkerchief from his pocket and offered it to Tave. "You want to use this?"

She nodded and took it from his hand. "There's a well in back of the church. Let's go draw some water so I can wash my face and hands. I'll worry about my dress later."

Tave glanced over her shoulder on the way to the well. The girls had already resumed their game. She glanced at Daniel. "Now you have a small sample of what my day as a teacher is like."

He smiled at her. "I wish I'd had a teacher like you when I was a child."

They reached the well, and within minutes, Daniel had lowered the bucket and drawn cool water from the dark depths. A dipper hung on a peg at the side of the well, and Tave filled it with water and poured it over Daniel's handkerchief.

She wiped at her face then turned to him. "Do I have all the dirt off?"

He laughed and took the handkerchief from her. "There's a little bit left on the side of your face. Let me get it for you."

He stepped closer and bent forward as he wiped at her face. She closed her eyes and lifted her face. When he drew his hand away, she opened her eyes and stared up at him. His blue eyes stared into her, and in their depths she detected a longing that equaled the one she felt. His gaze went to her lips and lingered there.

A thrill raced through her at the thought of their lips meeting. She reached up and cupped his face with her hand. "Daniel," she whispered.

He pulled her closer, and her heart almost beat out of her chest as she waited for his kiss. Before their lips met, he groaned and backed away. "No, Tave," he muttered. "I won't do this."

He released her with a slight shove, and a chill raced through her at the anger she detected in his eyes before he whirled and strode toward the far side of the church. Speechless, she stared at Daniel's back.

It only took Tave a few seconds to recover and dash after Daniel. She caught up with him at the cemetery and grabbed his arm. "Daniel, what's the matter with you? You looked at me like you hate me. What have I done?"

He stopped and whirled to face her. "You haven't done anything. I did. I almost kissed you. That would have been the biggest mistake of my life."

"Mistake?" She shrank from him. How could he say such a terrible thing? She wrapped her arms around her waist and blinked back tears. "Are you telling me you don't have any feelings for me?"

He raked his hand through his hair and groaned. "I do have feelings for you, but I'm not going to take advantage of you and give you false hope."

"False hope about what?"

"That anything's ever going to come of it. I'm not the man for you, Tave."

She straightened to her full height. "Don't I get to decide that on my own?"

He shook his head. "No. I'm going to decide it for you. I'm a drifter with no money or family. I want you to understand I have nothing to give you."

She stared at him. "Can you give me love?"

His eyes grew wide. "Wh-what?"

She squared her shoulders and clenched her fists at her sides. "Savannah told me she could tell that you're in love with me. As embarrassing as it is for me to ask, I have to know. Do you love me?"

He hesitated for a moment, and she held her breath. His shoulders drooped as if his whole body had deflated. "Yes, I love you. More than I ever thought it possible to love someone else."

Her heart pounded, and she frowned. "Then what's the problem? I've fought my feelings for you, but I can't anymore." She stepped closer. "I love you, too, Daniel."

He held up his hands as if to warn her to stay back. "No, I won't saddle you with a man who can't give you everything that Matthew can."

"Matthew? What does he have to do with this? I don't love him. I love you."

He reached out and grabbed her by the shoulders. "It doesn't matter. I won't keep you from the life you deserve." He released her with such force that she stumbled back. "I have to leave."

Icy fear gripped her. "Leave?"

"Yes. When I'm gone, you'll know I was right."

Tave watched in disbelief as he headed toward the road. She ran after him and grabbed his arm. "Where are you going?"

He shook free of her. "I'm going back to your father's office right now. I think it would be better if we stayed away from each other until it's time for me to leave Willow Bend. I told Mr. Perkins I'd be at work tomorrow, and I won't go back on my word. I'll help him a few weeks; then I'm going to pack my belongings, get on my new horse, and go on to Montgomery."

"Please don't do this to me, Daniel."

He turned back to her, and Tave's heart broke at the agony in his face. "I'm doing it *for* you, Tave, not *to* you. From the very beginning, I've been honest with you. I can't stay anywhere very long before I get the urge to move on again. Sooner or later, I'd leave you, too. Matthew is here to stay, Tave. I'm not. You'll see that I was right."

It was no use. Nothing she could say would change his mind. She nodded. "All right. Run away, Daniel. That's what you always do. But before you go, there's something I want to say."

"What?"

She took a deep breath and prayed she'd speak the right words. "Matthew's not the problem. I think you're just using him as an excuse."

He shook his head. "I only want the best for you."

Anger welled up in Tave's heart, and it frightened her. She jutted out her chin and stepped closer to him. She hoped her eyes conveyed the fire she felt in her soul. "The problem is that you're a man who's given his life over to hate for so long that you don't know how to open up to love. You think the answer to your problem is to give up and run from the hate that's gnawed at your heart for the past seven years, but it hasn't worked because you just carry it with you to the next place. Maybe one day you'll finally see that you're never going to have any peace or be able to return anyone's love until you let God's love replace all the hate that's killing you."

Tave couldn't control the tears that puddled in her eyes any longer, and she whirled away from him before he saw them running down her face. She didn't look back as she walked toward the picnic grounds. Laughter echoed from the people who'd been her friends for years. She spied Savannah talking with some women, but she didn't want to see her now. There was only one place she wanted to be.

She stepped onto the porch of the church and went inside.

❧

Two weeks later on a hot July morning Tave sat in the shade of a tree in the backyard of their house. A pan of tomatoes sat at her feet, and she tapped the metal pot with the toe of her shoe. She'd picked the tomatoes from her garden and planned on canning them, but for some reason, she was restless today. Maybe it was because she hadn't spoken to Daniel since the day of the picnic.

He didn't come to meals at their house anymore, and she stayed away from her father's office and Mr. Perkins's store. When her father mentioned Daniel, she changed the subject.

She thought about how few people she'd seen lately. Savannah had come by once or twice, but Tave couldn't bring herself to discuss her heartbreak with her friend, who had such a wonderful husband and family. This was a burden she was going to have to bear alone. She hadn't even been able to share it with her father. Tave could see the concern in his eyes, and he kept asking her what was troubling her. She kept hoping Daniel would come to see her, but so far, he hadn't.

She sighed and bent to pick up the tomatoes. A familiar voice rang out. "Hello. Anybody home?"

Martha Thompson. Tave didn't know if she was up to a visit from the woman today, but she pushed to her feet. "I'm out back, Martha."

Martha shuffled around the side of the house and directed a grin in Tave's direction. "There you are. I was afraid you was sick. I ain't seen you around much lately. Anything wrong?"

Tave shook her head and pointed to the tomatoes. "No. I've just been busy with my garden."

Martha slapped her leg and laughed. "Landsakes! Don't I know about gardens. Me and Esther have 'bout worked ourselves to death with ours. It takes a heap of food when a family's got five children."

Tave nodded. "I can imagine it does."

Martha cocked her head and smiled. "I was just on my way home from Mr. Perkins's store and thought I'd check on you."

"Well, I'm glad you did. Would you like to have a cup of tea before you walk home?"

"No, I ain't got time. I've gotta get home and ask my boy Tad if he wants to go to work for Mr. Perkins. He needs some help, you know."

Tave's heart pounded in her chest. "No, I didn't know that."

"Oh yeah. That nice Mr. Luckett is leaving today. Going to Montgomery, he says. We sure gonna miss him around here." Martha's eyes narrowed, and she looked at Tave as if checking the effect her words produced.

Tave grabbed the back of the chair for support and tried to smile. "Yes, we are."

Martha continued to study Tave for a moment before she

glanced down at the tomatoes. "I'd better get out of here so's you can get to work. Just wanted to say hello."

The woman turned and walked from the backyard. It took Tave a moment to collect her thoughts. She raised her hand, waved, and called after her. "Thanks for stopping by, Martha."

When Martha had disappeared, Tave dropped down in the chair and buried her face in her hands. Anger washed over her, and she sat up straight. What was Daniel thinking? Was he just going to sneak out of town without even saying good-bye after all she'd done for him? No, he was going to face her and tell her good-bye.

She jumped to her feet, jerked off the apron she wore, and threw it in the chair. With her fists clenched at her sides, she stormed from the backyard and headed toward her father's office.

ten

Daniel had just stuffed the last shirt in the bag his clothes had arrived in from the *Montgomery Belle* when he heard the door of Dr. Spencer's office open. He froze in place and held his breath. Soft footsteps tapped across the wooden floor of the waiting room. They stopped outside the bedroom, and a knock sounded at the door.

"Daniel, are you in there?"

A relieved breath escaped Daniel's throat at the sound of Dr. Spencer's voice. At least Tave hadn't come to see him. He hoped he could get out of town without her knowing. "Yes, come on in."

The door swung open. Daniel pulled the drawstring that closed the top of the bag and turned. Dr. Spencer's gaze appeared riveted on the bag. He took a deep breath and looked up. "Is that your horse tied to the hitching post out front?"

"Yes."

He glanced down at the bag again. "So you're really leaving."

He nodded. "It's time I moved on." He pointed to the lamp table. "I was hoping you'd be back from Cottonwood before I left, but I wrote you a note in case you weren't."

Dr. Spencer rubbed his tired eyes. "It's been a long night. The wife of one of the tenant farmers had a baby. It took a long time, but everything turned out all right."

The front door of the building opened and slammed shut. Someone stomped across the waiting-room floor. Daniel's heart almost stopped when Tave appeared at the door to the bedroom. He couldn't tell if it was anger or hurt in her eyes, but he realized that whatever it was had to be directed at him.

Her chin trembled. "Martha tells me you're leaving."

He turned back to the bed and pretended to secure the top of his bag. "That's right."

Dr. Spencer cleared his throat. "I think I'll go into my office and let you two say your good-byes." He stopped beside Tave and patted her shoulder. "I'll be in the next room."

She bit her lip and nodded before her father left the room. After a moment, she inched closer. "Weren't you going to tell me you were leaving?"

Daniel pointed to the lamp table. "I left a note."

A strangled laugh came from her throat. "After all these weeks, I only get a note. You were going to leave without telling me good-bye."

He willed himself not to move toward her. He had to keep his distance. "You know why I couldn't see you."

"I know what you said, but I can't believe you'd leave town without at least thanking me for sitting by your bed and nursing you back to health, for cooking your meals, for—" She swallowed. "I suppose whatever else I might feel doesn't matter."

His heart told him to close the distance between them, to take her in his arms, and tell her he didn't want to ever be parted from her, but he didn't move. "Don't make this any harder than it already is, Tave. I'm going, and there's nothing you can say to change my mind."

"I guess I knew that when I came." She glanced at his packed bag and back to him. "Will you do one thing for me, Daniel?"

He swallowed. "What?"

She pointed to the lamp table where her Bible still lay. "Take my Bible with you and read it. Maybe you can find the peace you're looking for."

"If you want me to take it, I will."

She stepped back from him. "I want you to stick it down in your bag; then I want you to leave. I've done a lot of thinking in the past two weeks, and I've come to realize it would never have worked out for us. I want a man who can love me, not someone whose heart is shriveled up with so much hate that he's turned his back on God. If the day ever comes that you turn your life over to God and allow Him to take away all that hate, think of me, Daniel, a woman who loved you for the man she could see waiting to be released from the past. I'll think about you often, and I'll pray for you every day."

She whirled and ran out of the room. He wanted to go after her, but he knew he couldn't. She'd forget him in time.

Daniel closed his eyes and bit his lip. The front door slammed, and he realized he was alone again, just as he had been for years. A discreet cough at the edge of the room caused him to open his eyes. Dr. Spencer walked in and stopped at the foot of the bed. "Do you have everything you need?"

"Don't worry. I'll be fine."

Dr. Spencer frowned. "I hope so. Just be careful of your side for a while."

"I will."

Dr. Spencer pushed his glasses up on his nose and took a deep breath. "I saw Tave leave. She didn't ask me to stop you, and I won't try."

"Thank you. You couldn't change my mind."

"I know. If I've learned anything in this life, it's that you can't change folks from whatever they're bound and determined to do. Only God can do that."

Daniel's shoulders slumped, and he dropped down on the

bed. He clasped his hands between his knees and stared at the floor. "I don't want to go, but I feel like I have to."

Dr. Spencer eased down beside him. "Because of Tave?"

Daniel jerked his head around to stare at Dr. Spencer. "How did you know?"

He shrugged. "I thought something was wrong when she wanted to leave the picnic early that day. Then when we got home, she told me you were leaving and ran into her room. She's hardly gotten out of the house since then. I figured something had happened between the two of you."

Fear at telling Dr. Spencer what had happened washed over him, and Daniel averted his gaze. "Tave is a wonderful woman. She's too good for me. I can't give her the things that Matthew can, and she deserves to have a good life."

"Did you tell her that?"

"Yes."

"What did she say?"

Daniel swallowed before he spoke. "That she doesn't love Matthew."

Dr. Spencer laid his hand on Daniel's shoulder. "Do you love my daughter, Daniel?"

He bit his lip and nodded before he turned back to face Dr. Spencer. "With all my heart, but I'm not going to stay here and ruin her life."

Dr. Spencer rose, clasped his hands behind his back, and walked across the room before he stopped and retraced his steps. "You would ruin her life if you stayed."

Daniel thought he'd heard the doctor wrong. The realization that her father hadn't thought him good enough for Tave hit him like a kick in the stomach. All he could do was try to disguise his disappointment. "Then you think it's best for me to leave?"

Dr. Spencer peered over the rim of his spectacles. Sadness shadowed his eyes, and Daniel felt as if the man could see into the depths of his soul.

"I'm just a country doctor who's devoted his life to healing folks' ailments. Sometimes, though, I see someone who has a sickness that I can't do anything about, and I have to rely on a higher power to take over."

"You're talking about God."

Dr. Spencer nodded. "I am. Tave told me you've had a lot of bad things happen in your life, things that have hardened your heart and made you doubt God. She thought maybe you were beginning to see the truth, but I can tell you haven't quite reached that stage yet. So I think you're right about leaving. You and Tave never would be able to have a life together."

Daniel rose to his feet. "Thank you for seeing it my way."

Dr. Spencer held up his hand. "Hold on there, Daniel. I didn't say I see it your way. I said you were right to leave. By that I mean that Tave needs someone who has a deep faith in God, a man who'll turn his life over to Him and follow whatever path God leads him on. I don't want anything less than that for my daughter."

A frown pulled at Daniel's brow. "You mean you wouldn't mind the fact that I don't have any money or any prospects of getting any?"

Dr. Spencer sighed. "Daniel, there's a lot more to life than what money can buy. Jesus once spoke about that to a large group of people and told them to look at the lilies of the field and the sparrows in the air and see how God took care of them. He ended by telling the crowd not to worry about what they should eat or what they wear. Then He spoke some words that I carry with me every day. He said, 'For all these things do the nations of the world seek after:

and your Father knoweth that ye have need of these things. But rather seek ye the kingdom of God; and all these things shall be added unto you.'"

"What does that mean?"

"It means that when you open your heart to God's love, He's going to take care of you. You may never be rich, but when He's working through your life, those things aren't the most important anymore. We see other things that mean so much more."

Daniel nodded. "I've been reading the Bible, and I felt so peaceful when I went with you and Tave to church. Then I remember what happened to my mother, and I can't let go of the past. It's just too hard."

Dr. Spencer smiled. "It is for all of us. It was hard for me to let go of the terrible things I saw men do to each other during the war. If I hadn't put my faith in God, I don't think I could have survived that time. Until you come to the place where you can turn the past over to God, you're never going to have any peace. You've got an ache that I can't fix, but God can." He pointed to Tave's Bible on the table. "The best medicine for you is found in that book. Read it, Daniel, and let the words speak to your heart. Only then are you going to be ready to have a relationship with any woman."

Daniel stared at the Bible, walked over to the table, and picked it up. "Tave told me to take it with me."

"Then do it." Dr. Spencer stuck out his hand. "I'm glad I met you, Daniel, and I'm going to be praying you find the peace you need in your life."

They shook hands, and Daniel watched as Dr. Spencer walked from the room. He heard him cross the waiting room and the sound of the front door closing as he left. A vast emptiness consumed Daniel, and he staggered back. He'd left many places in the past and had never given it a thought. Now he knew he didn't want to leave the people he'd come to know here. He'd never felt more alone in his life.

What was it Tave had said to remember? The words flashed across his mind: *"If the day ever comes that you turn your life over to God and allow Him to take away all that hate, think of me, Daniel, a woman who loved you for the man she could see waiting to be released from the past."*

The urge to unpack his clothes overcame him, and he reached for the bag. He opened the top and reached inside, but stopped before he pulled out a shirt. "No!"

Gritting his teeth, he shoved the Bible in the bag, pulled the opening closed, and ran from the room. His horse waited outside at the hitching post. He tied the bag to the saddle horn, climbed on, and turned the horse north. It was time for him to go to Montgomery.

❧

Two days after Daniel left, Tave strolled down the main street of Willow Bend. She wondered where he was at that moment and if he was thinking of her. Tears flooded her eyes at the memory of their last conversation. She couldn't erase it from her mind.

She wiped at her cheeks and glanced around to see if anyone had seen her momentary lapse. No one appeared to be paying her any attention. Straightening her shoulders, she opened the door to Mr. Perkins's store and stepped inside.

At the sound of the bell over the door, Mr. Perkins hurried from the back room. His face lit up when he saw her. "Tave, come in. How can I help you today?"

She handed him the list she'd written before leaving home. "These are the items I need."

He scanned the list and nodded. "I have all this in stock.

I'll get it right away for you." He turned to walk to the other side of the store but stopped. "Oh, I almost forgot. The *Liberty Queen* docked today, and there was a letter for you."

A letter? Could it be from Daniel? Tave's heart pounded as Mr. Perkins strode to the counter at the back of the store that served as the post office for Willow Bend. An open cupboard with mailbox slots sat behind it. He pulled a letter from one of them, hurried back, and handed it to her.

"Here it is. Now if you'll excuse me, I'll go to the storeroom to get some of the items that are on your list."

"Thank you."

She held her breath and didn't move until he'd left the room. Her fingers shook as she raised the letter to get a better view of it. Tears sprang to her eyes, and her heart plummeted to her stomach. The letter wasn't from Daniel. It was from Matthew.

She grabbed the edge of one of the display tables to steady herself and bit her lip. After a moment, she took a deep breath and opened the letter. Her eyes widened with each word that she read. By the time she finished, her mouth hung open and her face burned.

Unable to believe what it said, she reread the words:

Dear Tave,

I feel the need to offer you an apology for my behavior the last time we talked. At that time, I mentioned the possibility of speaking to you of marriage when I returned. I realize now how presumptuous that was, because your father would never consent to our union. I also shouldn't have assumed that you would even consider such a proposal. Having reached this conclusion, I hope you will soon find some young man who will be worthy of your affection.

As for me, I have met such a woman in the person of Miss

*Portia Davenport of Dauphin Island. We will be married by
the time this letter reaches you. I look forward to introducing
you to my new wife when we arrive home.*

*Regards,
Matthew Chandler*

Tave crumpled the letter in her hand. "Of all the nerve," she
muttered. "Dismissing me like that. I've got a good mind to—"

She stopped midsentence and arched her eyebrows. What
was the matter with her? She didn't love Matthew. She hadn't
wanted to marry him and would have turned him down if he'd
asked. If she was honest, she'd have to admit the only thing
that was hurt was her pride. As her true feelings regarding
Matthew surfaced, a sense of relief flowed through her body.
She wouldn't have to worry about Matthew showing up to
relive the war and play checkers with her father anymore.

Glancing down at the wrinkled letter, she began to laugh.
She needed to go tell her father right away. "Mr. Perkins," she
called out, "I have to go to my father's office. I'll be back for
my purchases."

Without waiting for an answer, she ran out of the store
and up the sidewalk. She stopped outside her father's office
as another thought struck her. A few weeks ago, there had
been two men in her life, but she loved only one of them. All
she could do now was pray that somehow God would bring
Daniel back.

❧

Three days later, Tave sat in the parlor of Savannah's house at
Cottonwood Plantation. She studied the fragile china cup and
saucer with pink flowers painted on the sides before she took a
sip of tea and set it back on the serving tray.

"Thanks for inviting me this afternoon, Savannah. I don't

mind telling you this has been a hard week for me."

Savannah set her cup down and grasped Tave's hand. "I couldn't believe it when I heard Daniel had left. The two of you seemed so happy the day of the picnic."

Tave scooted back onto the sofa and propped a brocade-covered pillow behind her back. "It was such a wonderful day until I fell playing hopscotch."

Savannah reached for her cup and took another sip. "What happened?"

For the next few minutes Tave told her friend about the argument she and Daniel had after he almost kissed her. When she finished, she brushed a tear from her eye and tried to smile. "I didn't see him again until the day he left. I wouldn't have known he was leaving if Martha hadn't come by to tell me."

"Bound for Martha to bring the latest news."

Tave reached for one of the napkins on the tray and wiped at her eyes. She thought by this time all her tears would be gone, but they still popped out at unexpected moments. "In this case, I was glad she did. At least I got to tell him good-bye and give him my Bible to take with him. Poppa talked to him, too, before he left. Poppa hasn't told me what all was said, but he did say he told Daniel that he didn't think we could be happy together until he turned his life over to God."

Savannah nodded. "He's right, you know. Marriage is difficult even when you love each other. If two people aren't in agreement about God's place in their lives, it'll just bring unhappiness to both of them."

"I know. I've prayed about this, and I know everything is going to turn out all right for me. God's got something else in mind."

Savannah stood up. "Good for you. You don't need to waste

your time thinking about what might have been with Daniel Luckett. You need to occupy yourself with other interests." A coy grin pulled at her mouth. "Like Matthew."

Tave's eyes grew large. "Oh, that's right. You haven't heard, have you?"

"Heard what?"

"Last Tuesday when the *Liberty Queen* docked at Willow Bend, it brought a letter to me from Matthew."

Savannah reached to pick up the tray. "When's he coming home?"

Tave sighed. "I don't know. He wrote to apologize to me for speaking of marriage before he left for Dauphin Island. It seems he's met a young woman down there whom he's quite smitten by. He's going to bring her back as his wife."

The cups and saucers rattled as the tray slipped from Savannah's hands and thudded back to the table. She dropped back to the sofa, her eyes wide with surprise. "His wife?"

Tave laughed. "Yes." She tilted her head to the side and tapped her chin with her finger. "I wonder if I'm the only woman in Willow Bend who's ever lost two men within two days."

Red spots, a sign of her anger ever since Tave had known her, appeared on Savannah's cheeks. "Of all the nerve. He writes to tell you he's taking back his proposal. I can't believe he'd be such a coward."

"I have to admit it was quite a shock."

"Well, all I can say is good riddance to Matthew Chandler." Savannah grabbed Tave's hands. Her eyes brimmed with tears. "But I'm sure that makes the loss of Daniel only worse. I'm so sorry."

Tave squeezed Savannah's hands and shook her head. "Don't be. Neither one of them were meant to be. I wouldn't have married Matthew anyway, but. . ." She couldn't suppress the tears anymore, and she covered her face with her hands. Her body shook with sobs.

Savannah placed her arm around Tave's shoulders and drew her closer. Tave collapsed against Savannah's shoulder and cried out the hurt she'd tried to keep inside all week. Savannah patted her shoulder. "Go on and let it all out, Tave. It'll make you feel better."

She pulled back and wiped at the tears on her cheeks. "But I love Daniel so much. How can I get him out of my heart?"

Savannah shook her head. "I don't know. I shudder sometimes when I think how close I came to leaving Willow Bend and losing Dante. I believe God knew what was happening in our lives, and He made everything work out in the end."

A hiccup shook Tave's body, and she placed her hand over her mouth. When the urge had passed, she closed her eyes and sighed. It didn't seem possible that only a few months ago she'd been so happy. Now she wondered if she would ever smile again. "I've always said I believed God would lead me where He wanted me to go, but I never thought putting Him in control could be this hard. It sounds so easy to say you'll do it, but it sure does put your faith to the test."

Savannah leaned back on the sofa and drew Tave's head to her shoulder. "I know it's hard. God told us we'd have problems, but He promised He would be with us when we were passing through those times. Don't lose your faith, Tave. My aunt Jane once told me that God wasn't through with me, that He still had plans for me. I know He has the same for you."

"I'll try to hang on to that thought, Savannah. When things get bad, I'll think of what you said. I don't know what I'd do without you as a friend."

"Don't worry. You're going to be all right."

Tave's thoughts turned to Daniel. Surely he'd made it to Montgomery by now since it was only about three days away by horse. He was probably already working on the docks and making new friends. Some of them were probably women. Maybe he'd already forgotten about her. She wondered if she would ever forget him. She breathed a silent prayer for him.

❧

Daniel walked into the second-floor room he'd rented in a house close to the docks and tumbled onto the unmade bed. The late-afternoon September sun cast a shadow across the floor. He opened the small window in an effort to get some air into the hot room. He needed to rest. He hadn't slept well in the two months since he'd arrived in Montgomery, and the oppressive heat would probably keep him awake all night. His only consolation was that fall would soon arrive with cooler weather.

Before he'd climbed the steps to his room, Mrs. Whittaker, who owned the boardinghouse, had called out that supper would be ready in an hour. He didn't know if he could eat or not.

A soft knock at the door caused him to sit up. Even though he was sure he knew who stood there, he called out anyway. "Who is it?"

"It's Jacob Whittaker, Daniel. I thought I'd check on you."

There was something about Jacob that reminded Daniel of his grandfather who had died when he was young. Like his grandfather, Jacob never missed an opportunity to share his love for God and His Word.

Daniel opened the door and smiled at the white-haired, elderly man facing him. Pain pinched his face, and he leaned heavily on a cane. Daniel opened the door wider. "Come in, Mr. Whittaker. I didn't think you saw me come in."

Jacob hobbled into the room and sank into the chair next to a small table by the open window. "I was in the kitchen, but I heard my daughter-in-law speaking to you. I thought I'd come up here and see if you did what I asked."

Daniel glanced at the table beside Jacob. Tave's Bible sat on it. Picking it up, he opened it to the passage Jacob had told him about and read aloud. "'Love your enemies, bless them that curse you, do good to them that hate you, and pray for them which despitefully use you, and persecute you; that ye may be the children of your Father which is in heaven: for he maketh his sun to rise on the evil and on the good, and sendeth rain on the just and on the unjust.'"

Jacob planted his cane in front of him, rested his hands on top of it, and closed his eyes. "Beautiful words."

"Love your enemies?" Daniel asked. "How is that possible?"

"It's only possible if God has control of your life. The day you walked in our front door, I told my daughter-in-law you were a man with deep scars. Over the last two months, you've shared your past with me. I know you've suffered, but you can overcome it. You're never going to be happy until you let go of the hate in your heart."

"Someone else told me that, but she made it sound so easy."

Jacob's eyebrows arched. "Ah, a young woman told you the same thing I've been telling you ever since you've been in Montgomery. She's right. All you have to do is pray and ask Jesus to take control of your life. He'll take away the hate and replace it with peace." Jacob closed his eyes again and breathed deeply. "I can feel His presence every time I come into your room, Daniel. He's here, waiting for you to open your heart to Him."

Daniel looked back at the words he'd just read. Love, bless, do good to your enemies? Why should he? The veil that had covered his mind for years parted, and the answer hit him like a kick in the stomach. So he could be a child of God.

Suddenly, everything Tave and her father had said and all of Jacob's words made sense to him. They had been trying to make him see how his life would be changed if he opened his heart to God.

He gasped aloud at the great wave of emotion that poured through his body. He closed his eyes and let his senses soar with the recognition of an emotion he'd never felt before. Was it really as easy as Jacob said? If it was, why did he hesitate? He dropped the Bible, fell on his knees, and buried his face in his hands. "God, help me. I can't carry this hatred anymore. Help me to let it go. I want some peace in my life. Show me what to do."

The Bible lay on the floor where he'd dropped it. He picked it up and stared at the page where it had fallen open. The words of a verse almost stood out from the page, and his skin prickled as he read it: *"And that he died for all, that they which live should not henceforth live unto themselves, but unto him which died for them, and rose again."*

He clutched the Bible to his chest. From his seated position, Jacob stared down at him. "How do you feel, Daniel?"

The greatest peace he'd ever known washed over him, cleansing every bit of hate from his body. With tears on his cheeks, he smiled. "Like a great weight has been lifted from my shoulders. I feel so light, I think I might be able to fly."

Jacob laughed. "I remember that's how I felt when I accepted Christ. What are you going to do now?"

Daniel stuck out his hand, and Jacob grasped it. "There's still a lot I don't understand, Mr. Whittaker. Will you teach me more about the Bible and God's ways?"

Tears stood in the old man's eyes. "There's nothing that would make me happier."

eleven

Daniel buttoned his coat in an effort to ward off the chill from the brisk wind that swept across the docks. With Christmas Eve only two days away, there wasn't much activity on the river, and most of the workers had already gone home.

He thought of his warm room at Mrs. Whittaker's boarding-house and shivered. If he wasn't on a mission right now, he would be sitting in the dining room, having a hot cup of coffee and a piece of apple pie with Jacob. His stomach growled, and he pushed the thought away. Eating would just have to wait until he talked with Mr. Smith, the owner of a riverfront warehouse.

As long as Daniel had been in Montgomery, Mr. Smith had been a regular Saturday visitor to his business. Regular until today, that is. Daniel had stood in the cold for hours, hoping the man would appear, but so far he hadn't.

He was just about to give up and go back to his room when he spied Mr. Smith's carriage coming down the street. A black man in a long coat and a top hat guided the horses along the cobblestone street toward the riverfront. Mr. Smith huddled in the backseat underneath a heavy buggy rug.

The carriage pulled to a stop in front of the warehouse. With slow movements, Mr. Smith pushed the lap covering to the seat beside him and heaved his portly body up. He grunted as he stepped to the ground. Leaning on a cane, he spoke to the driver, who nodded, and then he hobbled into the building. The man in the front seat of the carriage didn't move or look around as Daniel stepped from the docks and headed toward the building.

Daniel stopped at the door and said a quick prayer before he pushed the sliding door to the side and stepped into the musky darkness of the warehouse. The interior of the building with its huge floor space reminded Daniel of a cave. Very little cargo sat inside the building, but that didn't surprise Daniel. In the months since he'd been in Montgomery, he'd seen a drastic reduction in goods shipped by river. The railroads could deliver faster, and those who made their living on the river were beginning to worry how much longer their businesses could survive.

Daniel glanced around and spotted the warehouse office to his left. The soft glow of an oil lamp cast a shadow underneath the office door and sent flickering patterns rippling across the floor. Overhead, more light filtered in through the small windows lining the top of the walls.

Daniel stepped to the closed office door and knocked. Footsteps shuffled inside before the door opened. The warehouse owner gripped the handle of his cane and propped himself erect. His eyebrows arched. "Yes? Can I help you?"

Daniel pulled off the hat he wore and held it in his hands. "Good afternoon, Mr. Smith. My name is Daniel Luckett. I wonder if I might have a word with you."

The man's gaze raked over Daniel, but he finally moved aside and motioned him to come into the office. He closed the door behind him and turned to Daniel. "Haven't I seen you working on the docks?"

Daniel nodded. "Yes, sir."

The man moved to a chair behind his desk and lowered himself into it. He motioned for Daniel to have a seat in a chair facing him. "What is it you want to talk to me about?"

Daniel sat down and scooted to the edge of the chair. He took a deep breath. "Mr. Jacob Whittaker told me that you are a good Christian man. I've come hoping you might help me with a problem I have."

Mr. Smith nodded and opened his desk drawer. "Oh, I see. You've heard that I'm the person a dockworker needs to come to when he has a problem." He pulled out a roll of money. "Do you need to buy food for your family for Christmas?"

Daniel's eyes grew wide, and he held up his hands and shook his head. "No, sir. I don't want your money. It's quite another matter."

A puzzled expression crossed the man's face as he stuffed the money back into the drawer and closed it. "Then what is it you need?"

Daniel cleared his throat. "Well you see, sir, a few months ago, I accepted Christ as my Savior, and Mr. Whittaker has been teaching me about the Bible. A few of the men who live at the same boardinghouse saw us reading the Bible, and they began to ask questions. Mr. Whittaker encouraged me to start a Sunday morning Bible study in my room. Then some other fellows heard about it, and they came, too. Soon, we'd outgrown my room, and we had to use the boardinghouse dining room. But sometimes we have to finish early so Mrs. Whittaker can serve the noon meal."

Mr. Smith chuckled. "How many do you have attending now?"

Daniel wrinkled his brow and mentally counted the men who'd been attending regularly. "About ten or twelve, but this week I had four more men tell me they'd be there tomorrow. The problem is we need another place to meet."

Mr. Smith stared at him. "But how can I help you?"

Daniel glanced over his shoulder. "Well you see, sir, I asked the men if they'd like to start going to a regular church, but they said they didn't think they'd fit in at a city church. They want to keep our group together. You have a mighty big warehouse here. I wondered if you would let us meet here for Sunday services. We wouldn't bother anything, and we'd clean up after ourselves. I'd be glad to pay you each week when I get paid."

Mr. Smith picked up a pen from his desk and studied it for a moment before he looked back at Daniel. "No need for you to pay me anything. I'll be glad for you to hold services here." His gaze wandered over Daniel. "So you're a preacher?"

Daniel frowned and shook his head. "No. I'm just a man who's learned a lot from Mr. Whittaker, and I promised God I'd go wherever He led. These men have a real hunger in their hearts to hear God's Word. Some of them are far from home, and they're lonely. They need to know that God can give them peace."

"It appears Mr. Whittaker has taught you well."

Daniel nodded. "Yes, sir, he has, and I'm still learning. But God did a miracle in my life, and I have to tell other people about it."

Mr. Smith leaned back in his chair and smiled. "Well, tell your friends to come here tomorrow and every Sunday afterward for services. You're welcome to use my warehouse as long as you need it."

Daniel stood up and backed toward the door. "Thank you, Mr. Smith. Mr. Whittaker said you were a kind man who loves the Lord. I appreciate your helping us out."

Mr. Smith held up a hand to stop him. "Tell me, Mr. Luckett, do all of the men have Bibles?"

"No, sir, but the ones who do share with the others."

Mr. Smith's stubby finger tapped on his desk for a moment.

"Tomorrow when you get here, there will be a box filled with Bibles inside the front door. Tell every man who doesn't have one to take one as a Christmas present from me."

Daniel couldn't believe what he'd just heard. He shook his head in disbelief. "I've been praying I could find enough Bibles for all the men to have one. I shouldn't be surprised when God answers my prayers, but I still am."

"That's a natural reaction we all have, because we can't begin to understand God's love." Mr. Smith glanced down at his desk and then motioned for Daniel to leave. "Well, go on now. I have some work to do. I hope you have a good service tomorrow, and tell the men I wish them a merry Christmas."

Daniel grinned. "I'll tell them, and I hope you have a merry Christmas, too."

Daniel pulled his hat on and hurried from the building. When he was on the street again, he stuck his hands in his pockets and stared up into the sky. "Thank You, Lord. You've provided for us again."

He whistled a tune he'd heard one of the men singing the other day, a song of the river, the man had said. For some reason, the melody made him think of Tave. He wondered what kind of Christmas she was going to have. She was probably married to Matthew by now and planning a celebration at her new home.

The memory of her smile and her long auburn hair stirred a longing in him that he knew would never go away. He wished he could tell her she was right about how he needed God in his life. He'd started to write her several times to tell her God had brought peace into his heart, but each time he'd torn up the letter and thrown it away.

It would do no good to stir up old memories. She had a new life now, and he prayed she was happy.

❧

Tave left Mr. Perkins's store and hurried toward her father's office. Christmas Eve was only two days away, and she still had so much to do. She'd baked the jam cakes yesterday, but she still had to make the gingerbread she'd promised to take with them to Cottonwood on Christmas Day. She also had to finish the scarf she was knitting for her father to wear when he made house calls outside of town in cold weather.

She rushed through the doorway of her father's office. "Poppa, are you here?"

He appeared from the small kitchen, a cup in his hand. "I'm right here. Would you like to join me for some coffee?"

Tave shook her head. "I don't have time. I've been over to Mr. Perkins's store. Savannah was there, and she reminded me that we needed to be out at Cottonwood in time for Christmas dinner on Tuesday."

"Did you tell her we wouldn't miss it?"

She laughed. "I did. She said she and Mamie are planning a feast. My mouth watered just listening to her talk."

Her father smiled and motioned for her to follow him into the kitchen. "I just put some wood in the cookstove. It'll be warmer in here."

They sat down at the table, and Tave glanced around the room. Since school had started, she'd had little time to come by her father's office except for quick visits to check on him. She had hardly been in this room since she'd last cooked the meals that she, her father, and Daniel had shared.

Her gaze fell on the dry sink, and she recalled how Daniel's hand had once touched hers while standing there. Her chest tightened, and she blinked to keep tears from forming in her eyes.

Her father leaned forward, a worried expression on his

face. "What's the matter? Don't you feel well?"

She laughed and touched the corner of her eye. "It's nothing."

He took a sip of his coffee and set the cup back on the table. He reached across the table toward her. "We don't talk much about Daniel, darling, because I don't want to upset you. But I want you to know that I'm here for you anytime you need me."

She smiled and patted his hand. "I know you are. Having you and Savannah to give me moral support has gotten me through these past months." She sighed and pressed her fingertips to her temples. Closing her eyes, she tried to massage away the pain that seemed to hover at the back of her eyes all the time. "For a long time, I kept thinking he'd come back, but I'm about to give up hope."

"Do you want him to come back?"

She'd asked herself that question many times. "I don't want him to come back the way he was. I keep praying that something we said finally got through to him, and that he's changed. If he has, then I hope he does."

Her father's forehead wrinkled. "How long are you going to wait? I don't want to see you waste your life, hoping for something that may never happen."

"I know you don't, but I can't answer your question. My heart's not ready to give up on him yet."

Her father grinned. "Well, I have to admit I haven't had to go looking for opponents who want to beat me at checkers. There've been several young men who'd like to get to know you better. I especially like Joshua Tucker. He's not much of a checkers player, but he loses well."

"Joshua is a good friend, and I've enjoyed getting to know him. That's as far as it will ever go with us." Tave crossed her arms and rolled her eyes. "But you needn't worry about me ever finding a husband. I'm never going to get married because you scare off all the men by crushing their spirits when you beat them."

He laughed and pushed to his feet. He came around the table, placed his hand on her shoulder, and kissed her on the cheek. "I'm glad you can joke about it, darling. But I can see in your eyes that your heart is broken over Daniel. I wish I could help you, but I can't."

She turned her head and kissed his hand. "Thank you for caring, Poppa. I don't know what I'd do without you."

The bell over the front door of the office jingled, and a man's voice called out. "Doc, you here?"

Her father sighed. "It sounds like I have a patient. You go on home, and I'll see you there."

Tave waited until her father took the man into his office and closed the door. Then she stood up, picked up her basket, and walked to the bedroom where Daniel had lain when he was so ill. She stood in the door and recalled the times she'd prayed beside his bed.

A longing to see him ripped through her, and she grasped the door frame to keep from collapsing. "Oh, God," she whispered, "when am I going to stop missing him?"

She stared into the room for a few more minutes, and then she squared her shoulders and left the building. As she passed the livery stable, Mr. Jensen waved to her from the corral. "Merry Christmas, Miss Spencer."

She smiled and waved back. "Merry Christmas to you, Mr. Jensen."

Christmas had always been her favorite time of year since she was a child. This year, though, she felt no joy in her heart. It had disappeared the day Daniel Luckett rode out of Willow Bend.

twelve

July had come again and with it the blazing heat that threatened to cause every plant and blade of grass to shrivel and die.

Tave could hardly believe a year had passed since Daniel's departure. Another school year had drifted by, and the summer break was half over. There hadn't been much excitement in Willow Bend in the last twelve months unless she could count the June wedding of Esther Thompson to Joshua Tucker, Tave's friend and a tenant farmer out at Winterville Plantation. Martha hadn't quit talking about her new son-in-law for weeks, but everybody else went about their business, content to let one day blend into another. Before Tave knew it, she was one year older.

Sometimes one of her students would remind her of the day she fell playing hopscotch, and she would smile as they recalled last year's church picnic. At times, thoughts of Daniel would flash through her mind and be gone before she had time to dwell on them. At other times, the memory of his deep blue eyes and the way her skin had tingled the day he almost kissed her would sweep over her and leave a desolate emptiness in her heart. Today was one of those times.

The thoughts had probably been brought on by her task of cleaning the patient bedroom at her father's office. The patchwork quilt had been taken back to their house months ago, and she had packed it away. She couldn't stand to see the covering—a reminder of another time in her life.

With a sigh, Tave grabbed the broom she'd brought into the room and began to whisk it back and forth across the wood floor. Work was what she needed. Anything to take her mind off the memories this room evoked.

The front door opened, and her father's familiar footsteps echoed through the empty building. "Tave? Are you here?"

She stepped from the room and smiled. He'd been gone all night, and the rumpled shirt and trousers he wore told her he'd been busy. "I was beginning to worry about you."

He set his medical bag on a table, dropped down in a chair, and closed his eyes. "I'm exhausted. I've been to three different farms along the river since I left here yesterday afternoon."

Tave set the broom aside and hurried to stand behind him. Placing her hands on his shoulders, she rubbed the tight muscles as she often did when he was so tired. "Three? That's a lot of families to have sickness at one time."

He nodded. "Yes, and I'm afraid they're just the beginning."

Tave's body tensed, and her fingers stilled. "Why? What's the matter?"

"Yellow fever," he whispered.

Tave flinched at the words that could cause panic in the strongest of hearts. She pulled her hands from her father's shoulders and walked around the chair to face him. "Yellow fever? Are you sure?"

He rubbed his hands across his eyes. "I wish I wasn't."

She swallowed back the fear building inside her. "How many cases so far?"

"Two at a tenant farmer's home at Cottonwood, one over at the new Oak Hill owner's house, and Mrs. Somers."

Tave could barely believe what her father was saying. "Are any of them critical?"

"The only one who is right now is Mrs. Somers. I don't

know what made them wait so long to let me know. Reverend Somers said she kept telling him she was going to be all right. By the time I got there, she had already developed jaundice."

"Oh no." Tave's mind raced at what the next few weeks could bring to their quiet little town. "Do you think I need to go over to help with Mrs. Somers?"

Her father jerked upright in the chair, and his eyes widened in fear. "No. You need to stay away from any of the sick. I don't want you coming down with this."

She smiled and patted her father's hand. "If I remember correctly, you're the one who's always believed this terrible disease is caused by some kind of insect, a gnat you said."

He nodded. "I know. But I've been ridiculed by every medical group I've ever presented my theory to. Until somebody finds out the real cause of it, I want you to take every precaution." Tears filled his eyes. "You're all I have in this world, and I couldn't stand it if something happened to you."

"And neither could I if you became ill. You're the one who's going to be with all these sick people. I'd think you'd be more at risk than I would be."

He sighed. "If this becomes an epidemic, and I pray it won't, I may need you. But not until that time. Do you understand?"

She leaned over and kissed him on the cheek. "Yes. Now I want you to lie down on the sofa in your office and get some rest. I'll stay here in case someone comes for you."

He pushed to his feet. "I think I'll do that." He walked toward the door to his office but stopped and turned toward her before he entered. "Tave, please pray that we'll only have a few isolated cases."

She smiled. "I will, Poppa."

The look in his eyes, however, told her that he didn't think they'd escape this disease so easily. She had the feeling dark days awaited the residents of Willow Bend.

❧

A week later, Tave knew she'd been right. Nearly every home along the river had reported at least one case of yellow fever. Her father was nearing exhaustion from little sleep, but he wouldn't refuse any call for help. With the death toll at fifteen, the first being Reverend Somers's wife, and more cases being reported every day, he moved like he lived in a dream world.

Tave glanced around her father's office that had been converted into an emergency hospital for the most serious cases. The community had responded to the call for beds, and all ten that had been donated were filled with patients. Tave didn't know where they would place the next victim. She prayed there wouldn't be another one.

The mothers of three patients hovered near the children's beds, and Tave was grateful for their help. Most people were afraid to venture into the midst of the disease. She'd found herself giving aid to the other seven people near death.

She had even become immune to the stench in the room from the constant vomiting of those so sick. It never ceased to amaze her how much strength God could provide when it was needed.

A whimper from one of the beds caught her attention, and she hurried to kneel beside an elderly man who lived alone in a small house at the edge of town. He didn't mingle with the town folks much and appeared to live off his garden and the fish he caught in the river.

As Tave bent over him, she realized how she'd failed in the past to make an effort to know this man. Maybe he'd lived a lonely life, waiting and hoping for someone to act as if they cared. She wet a cloth and rubbed his face.

He opened his eyes, and Tave flinched at the yellow tint that had even invaded his pupils. She reached for a glass of rice-water on the table beside his bed. She lifted his head from the pillow and placed the glass on his lips, but he was unable to drink. Lowering him, she picked up a spoon and began to feed him the water.

She'd just completed the task when the front door opened. She glanced over to see Savannah and Mamie Clark walking inside. Tave jumped up and rushed across the room. "What are you two doing here?"

Savannah pulled her bonnet from her head and her nostrils flared. For a moment, Tave thought Savannah was going to be sick, but she straightened her shoulders and turned a determined look on Tave. "From the looks of things, you and your father need some help. Mamie and I have come to volunteer."

Tave shook her head. "No, you can't do that. You have children to take care of. What if you get sick?"

Savannah waved her hand in dismissal. "Mamie and I had this conversation with Dante and Saul. We can't go through life being afraid of what might happen. We have to trust God to take care of us. We're here to do His work with these people in need."

Mamie smiled, and her eyes lit up her dark face. "Miss 'Vanna's right. We gwine help any way we's can. So jest tell us what needs a-doin'."

Tave grasped their hands. "Thank you so much. Come with me. I'll show you."

She led the way to the kitchen and explained how they were treating the patients with plenty of liquids, the only known treatment to counteract the fluids they were losing from vomiting. "They're all running high fevers, and they're restless from aching muscles. Poppa says we should keep cool cloths on their heads and try to get some liquids down them. We're using black tea with a little sugar in it and rice-water. We need to keep a supply of each of those." Mamie nodded. "I kin take care of that."

Tave took two aprons from the pegs by the stove and handed one to each of the women. "Savannah, are you sure you're up to this? Some of the patients are still in the acute stage of the disease. They're running fever and having terrible aches with some vomiting. The ones in the toxic stage are much worse. In addition to the vomiting, some of them are hemorrhaging. This is not going to be an easy task."

Savannah tied the apron around her waist and took a deep breath. "Don't worry about me. I'm ready to help."

"Then come with me." Tave led her friend into the waiting room and directed her to the bed of a young woman who moaned aloud before Tave headed back to the bedside of the man she'd been helping. As Tave bent over him, she wiggled her shoulders. The back of her neck itched. She reached over her shoulder and scratched her skin then straightened. Just a mosquito bite—a summertime hazard of living on the river.

❧

"Hey, Preacher. We need you over here."

Daniel glanced over his shoulder at a group of dock-workers who stood at the gangway of a steamboat tied to the pier. Daniel walked toward the men he'd worked with and come to know in the past year.

"What can I do for you?"

One of the men pointed to the ship. "There's a sick man on board who's calling for a preacher. We told him we had one working on the dock."

Daniel chuckled. "Did you tell him I'm not a licensed preacher?"

The dockworker's eyes grew wide. "What difference does that make? You're the one that holds Sunday services over at that warehouse, and I ain't seen nobody else preaching except you."

Daniel nodded. "Sometimes I think you fellows railroaded me into leading the services in case none of you could show up after a night of living it up in that saloon all of you frequent."

A sheepish grin covered the face of Augie, the man Daniel had been trying to reach for the past six months. "Aw, Preacher, you know that ain't true. You're the only one who knows 'bout the Bible."

"Only because I study it, Augie." He glanced at the ship. "Now where is this man who wants a preacher? Maybe I can say something that will help."

Augie pointed to a cabin on the lower deck. "Right there, but you may not want to go."

"Why not?"

"They think he has yellow fever. They're waitin' for somebody to come take him off the boat. Nobody on board wants to touch him."

Daniel frowned. "Is he near death?"

Augie shrugged. "That's what they say."

A memory of being near death on a boat returned, and the faces of those who had helped him flashed into Daniel's mind. "Then he's in need of comfort." Daniel walked onto the boat, stopped at the door, and knocked.

The door was opened by a middle-aged woman. A worried expression covered her face. "Yes, may I help you?"

Daniel pulled the cap from his head and smiled. "I work on the docks, ma'am. Some of my friends said you were in need of a preacher. I'm not a licensed one, but I do hold services for the dockworkers every Sunday."

Her face relaxed into a smile. "My name is Lydia Collins. I think my husband, Herbert, may have caught yellow fever." She glanced over her shoulder. "He's very ill. I'll understand if you don't want to come inside."

Daniel stared past her at the writhing form on a bed across the cabin. "I'd be glad to come in if I can be of any help, ma'am."

She opened the door wider and smiled. "Then please come in. We've called for a doctor, but he hasn't gotten here yet. Herbert asked if I could find a preacher to pray with us. Thank you for coming."

Daniel stepped into the darkened cabin. The man groaned in agony, and his fingers clutched the side of the bed. Daniel knelt beside him and placed a hand on the man's trembling arm. "My name is Daniel Luckett. I've come to pray with you."

He nodded, and Daniel bowed his head. "Dear God, I come to You today on behalf of Herbert. He's in a great deal of pain right now and needs the assurance that he's not alone. Give him peace as only You can, and let him know that You are still in control. We can do nothing except place our lives in Your hands. Father, Your Word tells us there is a season for all things. We pray that this will be a season of rejoicing at Herbert's returned health. Be with this loving wife who stands ready to help her husband, and comfort her in this difficult time. We thank You for what You're going to do in Herbert's life today, and we give You praise, Lord, for loving us and caring for us. Amen."

Daniel opened his eyes, and Herbert Collins turned his head on the pillow. A weak smile curled his lips. "Thank you," he whispered.

The door opened, and the ship's captain ushered a small

man holding a medical bag into the room. Daniel rose and backed away from the bed as the doctor bent over Herbert.

A hand touched his arm, and he glanced at Lydia Collins, who stood beside him. "Thank you, Mr. Luckett. You were a great comfort to my husband and me today."

Daniel smiled. "I'm glad I could be of service." He looked back at Herbert. "Yellow fever is a bad disease. Do you have any idea where he might have caught it?"

She nodded. "Actually I do. We live in Selma, but we've stayed the past few weeks with our dear friend Reverend Thomas Somers in Willow Bend. He lost his wife to the disease."

Daniel reeled from her words. "Willow Bend? I know Reverend Somers. You say his wife died?"

"Yes, she was the first. There have been many more since then."

Daniel almost doubled over from the pain that ripped through his body at the thought of Tave in the midst of that illness. He struggled to speak. "Did you happen to meet Dr. Spencer while you were there?"

She nodded. "Yes, once. He was very busy with so many sick people in the area. Right before we left for home I heard he'd set up a hospital at his office for the worst cases."

"And his daughter? Did you hear of her?" He could hardly speak the words.

She shook her head. "I'm sorry. I didn't meet her. We went back to Selma and caught the boat to Montgomery because none of the steamboats are stopping at Willow Bend right now. My husband is the pastor at a church in Selma, and he was supposed to speak at a meeting of church leaders here."

Daniel backed toward the door. "I hope your husband recovers. I'll go and let you talk with the doctor now."

Daniel bolted onto the deck of the ship, rushed to the

railing, and grasped it. He couldn't believe what he'd just heard. Why hadn't he known about the yellow fever outbreak in Willow Bend? Surely it had been in the newspapers. Somehow he'd missed it.

He thought of Tave and wondered if she was all right. And her father. What about him? An uneasy feeling washed over him, and he knew he had to find out about them some way. How could he do it?

He lifted his eyes toward heaven and breathed a prayer for God to show him what to do. Just give him some assurance that she was all right.

A door to a cabin down the deck from where he stood opened, and a man stepped out. He glanced back inside and spoke in a loud voice: "You look beautiful enough. Now quit wasting time, and let's go. This boat's going to be ready to depart before I can get you onshore."

Daniel's forehead wrinkled. There was something familiar about the dark-haired man's profile. Where had he seen him before? He turned, and Daniel gasped in recognition. This was the plantation owner he'd seen at Dr. Spencer's office, the man interested in Tave—Matthew Chandler.

Matthew approached and glanced at Daniel. A slight frown wrinkled his brow. He stopped and stared at Daniel. "You look familiar. Have we met?"

Daniel swallowed and nodded. "Last summer in Willow Bend. I was a patient of Dr. Spencer's."

Matthew nodded. "Oh yes. I remember."

Daniel took a step forward. "I've just heard the news about the yellow fever outbreak there. How bad is it?"

Matthew sighed. "Terrible. I think about twenty people have died so far." He looked back over his shoulder toward the cabin he'd exited. "I took my wife to Selma so that we could board the boat there. We're going to stay in Montgomery until the epidemic is over."

Daniel breathed a sigh of relief. Tave was safe. "I'm glad to hear that. How is your wife?"

"She's fine."

"And her father?"

Matthew frowned. "How would you know her father?"

The question surprised Daniel. "He was my doctor."

Matthew laughed. "Portia's father isn't a doctor."

"Portia? I thought you married Tave Spencer."

Matthew shook his head. "Oh, that's right. I'd come to visit Tave the day I saw you there. No, it didn't work out for us." His eyes clouded. "I was very sorry to hear that she was ill."

Daniel felt as if he'd been slapped. "Sick? With yellow fever?"

Matthew nodded. "Right before we left, one of my tenant farmers went to town. When he came back, he told me Tave had gotten sick with yellow fever."

Daniel staggered back. "How bad was it?"

Matthew hesitated before he spoke. "I think she was near death."

Panic seized Daniel. "I've got to get to Willow Bend right away."

"I don't know how you'll do that. The disease is traveling upriver. I heard that this is the last boat Montgomery is allowing in, and they're setting up blockades to keep anyone from going south."

Daniel heard the words, but he didn't care. He turned and ran from the boat. No matter what it took, he had to get to Willow Bend. He prayed he wouldn't be too late.

thirteen

Tave groaned and tried to turn on her side, but it was no use. Her back hurt, and her head ached. She'd never felt so helpless in her life. A soft hand touched her forehead, and she opened her eyes. Savannah stood over her, a smile on her face.

"Are you awake?"

Tave tried to answer, but her throat was too dry. Maybe she could nod, but she didn't even have enough energy to move her head. There wasn't a place in her body that didn't hurt. Her eyes drifted closed.

Footsteps approached her bed, and she tried to smile. She would recognize her father's steps anywhere. She could sense his presence, and she felt him lift her arm. "Her skin is turning quite yellow. That means the disease is attacking the liver."

He sounded so sad, and she wished she could tell him everything was going to be all right. She tried, but she couldn't reopen her eyes.

"What do I need to do, Dr. Spencer?" Savannah's voice drifted into her ear.

"Just keep up the liquids. Everything that comes up has to be replaced with even more in hopes that some of it will get into her body."

"I'll do my best, Dr. Spencer."

A soft sob sounded, and she wondered if her father was crying. She'd never seen him cry. He was so strong.

"Thank you, Savannah. I don't know what I'd do without you."

They moved away from the bed, and a chill shook Tave's body. She waited for it to pass and tried to think of something to make her happy. Daniel's face drifted into her mind, and she smiled inwardly. She wondered where he was and if she'd ever see him again. She hoped so.

&

Augie held the reins of Daniel's horse and waited for Daniel to tie the saddlebags on the mare's flank. "Are you sure you want to do this, Preacher? I hear those barricade guards are shootin' before they ask any questions. Just 'cause it's midnight, don't make the mistake they'll be asleep. You most likely won't make it a few yards past them before you get a bullet in the back."

Daniel patted the horse and took the reins from Augie. "I've gotta try. Thanks for coming to see me off."

Augie pulled his cap down on his forehead and scowled. "Aw, don't go making such a fuss. I just wanted to see you one more time while you was still breathin'."

Daniel laughed and shook Augie's hand. "Thanks for everything, Augie. Tell all the fellows that I talked with Mr. Smith, and he's going to see that services continue at the warehouse. And I told the Whittakers not to hold my room." He gazed into the face of the man he'd been praying about for months. "If I don't make it back to Montgomery, I want you to know I'll never forget you, and I'll never quit praying for you."

Augie tilted his head to the side and studied Daniel with a probing gaze. "I'll remember you, too. I ain't never known anybody like you before. I'll think about all those things you've been talking to me about."

Daniel smiled. "Good. I've turned you over to Jacob now that I'm leaving. He wants to help you like he has me." He put his foot in the stirrup and swung himself into the saddle. "Good-bye, friend."

Augie backed away. "Now remember what I told you. Follow the river until you get out of town. Once you're past the barricade outposts, I reckon it'll be safe enough to get back on the road."

"I'll remember."

"And one more thing. It's gonna be dark out there in the woods along the river. It might be good for you to lead the horse. You don't want her to step in no holes. Last thing you need is a horse with a broken leg."

Daniel rested his arm on the saddle horn and gazed down at Augie. "You're beginning to sound like a mother hen."

Augie grinned. "Can't help it. I done come to think a lot of you. Be careful, Preacher. I hope your woman friend is all right."

Daniel nodded and urged the horse forward. He glanced up at the sky and said a prayer of thanks for the cloudy night. With the moon obscured, he might be able to blend into the shadows better. Now if the Lord would just provide his horse a clear path, everything would be all right.

Daniel rode through the deserted streets of Montgomery. The *clip-clop* of the horse's hooves sounded like a drumbeat to his ears, but no one stirred in the dark houses they passed. As he approached the outskirts of town, he guided the horse off the road and into the trees that lined the riverbank. He slowed the horse to a walk and peered into the darkness before them. After a few minutes, he pulled the horse to a stop and dismounted. Taking the reins in his hands, he pressed his weight into the ground with each step before he led the horse forward. Inch by inch they began a slow advance that would take them past the barricades.

Only once did Daniel pull to a stop. Voices drifted through the trees. He stood still, his hand gently stroking the horse that seemed to sense the nearby danger. She didn't move as Daniel's fingers gently calmed her.

After what seemed an eternity, the voices quieted, and he moved on downriver. Three hours later, the clouds parted, and the moon reflected on the rippling water of the Alabama River. Daniel looked for landmarks that he remembered from his days on the *Montgomery Belle* and spotted a scraggly tree he'd often seen on the riverbank. He breathed a sigh of relief. They had cleared the barricades and were well south of the city.

He led the horse back through the trees, and within minutes they were on the road he'd traveled when he came to Montgomery. He offered a silent prayer of thanks for safety through a dangerous night and urged the horse south. If all went well, he would soon be in Willow Bend.

≈

Someone was crying again, but Tave couldn't tell who it was. She tried to call out, but her throat refused to work. Voices echoed in her ears. It reminded her of how she used to yell into the depths of her grandmother's well and hear her voice vibrate.

"How is she?" someone asked.

"I think she's dying." That almost sounded like her father, but the voice trembled more than her father's.

"Is there anything I can do?"

"Pray, Savannah. That's all that will help now."

Relief washed over her. Savannah was here. Maybe she could comfort whoever was crying. No one should be sad today. She'd had a dream that had made her so happy. She'd seen Daniel again, and he wasn't angry anymore. The hatred was gone from his life.

She was glad. So glad. Now she wanted to go back to sleep and dream again.

❧

On the second day after leaving Montgomery, Daniel rode into Willow Bend. The town looked like a ghost town with no one on the deserted streets, and he wondered if he was too late. Maybe everyone had died.

He rode into the livery stable and was relieved when Mr. Jensen stepped from one of the stalls. Daniel dismounted, tossed the reins to the man, and grabbed his saddlebags. "I'm Daniel Luckett. You took care of my horse when I was here last summer. I need you to do that again. I'm going to Dr. Spencer's office, but I'll be back later to pay you."

Without waiting for an answer, he ran out the door and down the street toward the familiar building. When he charged onto the porch, he grabbed the doorknob. Fear like he'd never known gripped him, and he couldn't open the door. What if she was dead? How would he be able to forgive himself for the way he'd talked to her the last time he'd seen her? He should have told her how much he loved her instead of pushing her to marry someone else.

But that hadn't been God's plan. Daniel had come to understand that God had sent him to Montgomery so he could meet Jacob Whittaker. Alone with Tave's Bible in his small room at the boardinghouse, he had digested everything Jacob had told him about God, and it had given him a new life. Now he realized that he had to trust God to take care of him no matter what he found in Dr. Spencer's office. He took a deep breath and pushed the door open.

A sour stench overpowered him, and he almost stumbled backward to the porch. His stomach rumbled in protest, but he forced himself to walk into the room.

The neat waiting room he remembered now resembled a battlefield hospital. Beds, each occupied by a patient, sat side by side with narrow walk spaces between them. Low moans joined together in a deadly chorus that chilled him.

In disbelief, he took in the scene before him. A woman, a scarf covering her blond hair, leaned over one of the beds. She turned toward him. Surprise flashed in her tired eyes. "Daniel, what are you doing here?"

Daniel took off his hat and let his gaze wander over the beds again. "Hello, Savannah. I heard about the epidemic. I came to see if I could help."

She wiped her hands on a cloth and hurried across the room. "I'm so glad you're here. Dr. Spencer needs anybody willing to volunteer."

He studied the faces of the patients again, but Tave wasn't among them. He had to know about her, yet he was too frightened to voice the question. The brim of his hat curled between his clenched fists. "Tave? Where is. . . ?" He choked on the last word.

Savannah glanced toward the patient bedroom where he'd stayed just a year ago. "In there."

Daniel tried to take a step, but his legs felt as if they had large weights attached. His mouth thinned into a straight line, and he willed his body to move. Slowly, he made his way to the open door and peered inside.

She lay on the bed where he'd spent his days after surgery. Her face was obscured by the form of Dr. Spencer sitting in a chair next to her. Daniel eased across the room, stopped behind the man he'd come to respect during his time in

Willow Bend, and placed his hand on the doctor's shoulder.

Dr. Spencer swiveled in the chair and looked up into Daniel's face. The broken person staring at him wasn't the strong man who'd spoken to Daniel of God's love just a year ago. Dr. Spencer's eyes held a vacant look as if he'd witnessed unspeakable horror. Gray stubble covered his face, the result of days without shaving.

When he saw Daniel, tears came to his eyes, and he pushed to his feet. "Daniel, I can't believe it's you."

Daniel wrapped his arms around the man who'd been the closest to a father he'd ever known and hugged him. Dr. Spencer's slight frame shook, and Daniel wondered how much weight the doctor had lost.

Daniel released him and stared into his eyes. "How's Tave?"

A tear trickled from the corner of Dr. Spencer's eyes. "I think she's dying. I'm glad you got here in time."

Although he'd known he might hear those words, they still stabbed at his heart. He stepped around Dr. Spencer and gazed down at Tave. Her beautiful auburn hair fanned out on the pillow, and he remembered the first time he'd seen it. Her eyes were closed, but the yellow tint of her skin sent chills through him. Her mouth opened, and her body tensed in a violent contraction.

Dr. Spencer shook his head. "She's lost so much fluid there's nothing to expel anymore."

Daniel bit down on his lip and studied her for a moment. "Then we have to get more into her."

"We've tried over and over, but it's done no good. She loses everything we get down her throat."

Daniel glanced at Dr. Spencer out of the corner of his eye. The gaunt figure looked little like the robust man he had known last summer. Dr. Spencer might not have contracted yellow fever, but the dreaded disease had taken its toll on the man. "You look worn out. Why don't you go lie down? I'll take over here. Can you get me whatever you're feeding her and a spoon? I'll see what I can do."

Dr. Spencer rubbed his eyes and nodded. "I'll be right back."

When Tave's father had left the room, Daniel knelt beside the bed and took her hand in both of his. He leaned close and whispered in her ear. "Tave, it's Daniel. I've come back. If you can hear me, I want you to know that I love you more than I can ever tell you. I'm sorry I hurt you when I left, but God needed me to go away for a while. Now He's brought me home, and I need you here with me."

Tave's body twitched, but she didn't open her eyes.

Daniel grasped her hand tighter and bowed his head. "Dear God, please look down on this woman today and touch her body. If it's Your will, Father, purge her of this terrible disease and return her to the people who love her. And give me the strength to face whatever may come our way. I love You, Lord." His lips trembled, and he struggled to speak. From the bottom of his soul a desperate wail burst from his mouth. "Oh God! Please don't take her away from me. Not now." He pulled her hand to his chest and shook with sobs.

Behind him someone gasped, and he straightened to see Dr. Spencer and Savannah standing in the doorway. Dr. Spencer's face held a questioning expression. "Daniel, you're praying?"

Daniel wiped at his tears and pushed to his feet. "A lot has happened to me since I left here. I'm not the same person I was."

Dr. Spencer's eyes grew wide. "What happened?"

Daniel pointed to Tave. "She came into my life and showed me how to trust God. Then I met a man in Montgomery who wouldn't give up on me, either. The hate I had is gone, and

I have the peace I'd wanted for years."

Savannah frowned. "Then why didn't you come back? Tave's been unhappy ever since you left."

"I thought she had probably married Matthew, and I stayed where I thought God wanted me. The fellows I work with in Montgomery even call me Preacher because I conduct services for them every Sunday."

Dr. Spencer's mouth gaped open. "You're a preacher?"

Daniel shook his head. "Not a licensed one who's been ordained. But my friend Jacob Whittaker says he thinks God's already ordained me."

Dr. Spencer and Savannah exchanged surprised looks before they both smiled at Daniel. Dr. Spencer shook his head. "God sure does work in strange ways sometimes."

Daniel nodded. "That He does. It took me getting shot to make the most important decision of my life." He reached for the pitcher Dr. Spencer held. "Now you two go on about your work. I'll take care of Tave."

He turned back to the bed and sat down in the chair beside it. He leaned toward her and patted her hand again. "You took care of me when I was sick. Now it's my turn to help you, but you've got to do your part, too. Fight to live, Tave. I need you."

Setting the pitcher on the bedside table, he dipped the spoon in, filled it, and lifted her head with his free hand. Slowly he brought the spoon to her mouth and forced it between her lips. Half of it trickled down the side of her face, but a sip went down her throat.

Daniel shook his head in disappointment before he reached for the pitcher and refilled the spoon. He had no idea how long it would take to get a sufficient amount of liquid into her body, but he knew it didn't matter. As long as she was breathing, he wouldn't give up.

fourteen

Twenty-four hours later, little had changed in Tave's condition. Daniel pulled himself up from the chair where he'd sat since arriving and stretched. Footsteps at the door caused him to turn.

Savannah stood there, a pan of water in her hands. "Mamie has some food in the kitchen. Why don't you get something to eat while I bathe Tave?"

He stared down at her, unwilling to leave. "She's better, don't you think?"

Savannah put the pan on the table next to the bed and placed her hand on Tave's forehead. "She does seem cooler." She looked up at Daniel. "I know she'd be so happy to have you here. She's missed you this past year."

Daniel nodded. "I've missed her, too. I almost came back once. I wanted to tell her she was right, that I had found God and I was at peace. But then I knew I couldn't stand to see her married to someone else."

"And all that time she was waiting for you to return. Well, you're here now, and she would be happy to know you've been preaching in Montgomery."

Daniel's face grew warm. "It's not really a church. Just a group of workers who need a place to worship."

"And you've been leading them. I'm very proud of you, Daniel."

"Thank you." Loud sobs rang out from the waiting room, and Daniel turned to see where they were coming from. "Who's that?"

"Martha Thompson. Her son Tad has taken a turn for the worse."

"Oh no." Daniel walked to the door and glanced into the room.

Martha Thompson, trying to force liquids down her son Tad's throat, sobbed with each sip he took. "There now, Taddy boy, you open your mouth for Mama. You gonna feel better when you drink this."

Daniel walked over to Tad's bed and touched Martha's shoulder. "How is he, Mrs. Thompson?"

She looked up at Daniel with stricken eyes, clamped her teeth onto her bottom lip, and shook her head. Tears rolled down her cheeks.

Daniel kneeled beside her. "We just have to keep praying."

Martha nodded. "I know." She stared back at her son. "He's such a good boy. He works so hard to please his daddy. And he's smart, too. I always wished he had the chance to do something more than farm. He used to say he was gonna be a doctor when he grew up. Now I just want him to have the chance to grow up." Her body shook with sobs.

Daniel took her hand in his. "Then let's pray for that, Mrs. Thompson."

They bowed their heads, and Daniel began to pray: "Dear Lord, we come to You with heavy hearts because of all the suffering and death the good folks of Willow Bend have seen. I pray that You will give us peace to face what may be ahead of us. Bless this dear mother, Father, who watches beside the bed of her son. Give her strength, and I pray that You will touch Tad and restore him to those who love him so much. We pray that You will lift this dreaded disease from our midst and heal those who are ill. These things we ask in Your name. Amen."

When he'd finished, Martha looked up at him. "Thank you, Daniel, for praying for my boy."

He squeezed her hand. "Savannah is bathing Tave. If you need me, I'll be in the kitchen."

She smiled. "When I saw your face that day they brought you up the bluff to Doc's office, I thought you was gonna die. I'm glad the Lord saved you. You've been a blessing to me today."

Her words pricked his heart. "And everybody in this town has been a blessing to me. Being shot was well worth what I gained from coming to Willow Bend."

He stood and started to the kitchen, but a whimper from another bed caught his attention. He walked over and stared down at the young man lying there. Dropping to his knees, he began to pray for him. When he'd finished, he went to the next bed and the next until he had prayed beside every bed in the room.

Only then did he make his way to the kitchen.

❧

Tave wanted to open her eyes, but they wouldn't obey her. She didn't feel like struggling anymore. She would just lie there and try to understand the sounds around her.

Something cool touched her head. It felt so good. "You look so pretty today with that clean gown on."

Tave's heart beat faster at the familiar sound. Savannah was with her.

A foggy memory returned. Someone else had been with her, and she tried to remember what was said. *I need you.* Now she remembered.

Someone needed her. But who?

She couldn't worry about that now. It hurt her head to think. All she wanted was to sleep.

Three days later, Daniel stood at the foot of Tad Thompson's bed. Martha alternated between spooning broth into her son's mouth and squeezing his hand. She glanced up at Daniel, and he thought he'd never seen a happier expression on anyone's face. He wished he could have seen that from others who'd had loved ones in Dr. Spencer's office. Since he'd been there, two of the patients had died.

He glanced toward Tave's room, where Savannah sat with her. Dr. Spencer thought her condition had improved some in the past few days, but she still hadn't opened her eyes.

Daniel rubbed his hands over his face and sighed. He had slept very little since returning to Willow Bend, but he wanted to be awake in case Tave regained consciousness.

"Ain't he lookin' good?" Martha's voice broke into his thoughts.

Daniel glanced at Tad and nodded. "He is indeed."

Tad squirmed as his mother squeezed his hand once more. "Aw Ma, I'm all right now. You don't have to keep carryin' on so."

Martha leaned over and kissed Tad on the cheek. "Well, I know when we get back home and you're back to your normal self, you won't let me fuss over you none. So while I got you flat on your back, I'm gonna take advantage of the situation."

Daniel's heart filled with gratitude to God that Martha had her son back. "Tad, I lost my mother when I was just a little older than you are. Don't ever take yours for granted. You're a very lucky boy to have someone who loves you so much."

Tad grinned and winked at Daniel. "I know. I just like to give her a hard time sometimes."

Martha laughed and stood up. "Landsakes, this boy is

something else. Takes after his father. They both just love to tease me." She reached over and smoothed Tad's hair. "Now I'm gonna take this bowl back to the kitchen and get me something to eat. I'll be back before long."

"Take all the time you need, Ma. I'm not goin' anywhere."

Daniel watched Martha leave before he glanced back at Tad. "I'm glad you're doing so much better."

"Thanks, Mr. Luckett." He glanced toward the other room. "How's Miss Spencer?"

"About the same."

Tad settled back on his pillows, and a smile pulled at his lips. "Do you remember when Miss Spencer fell playing hopscotch?"

The memory of their argument after the incident flashed across his mind, and he nodded. "Yes. That was at the picnic."

Tad's eyes clouded. "She's such a good teacher. I sure hope she gets better."

Daniel sighed. "So do I."

"You know," Tad continued, "Pa had told me I couldn't go to school last year. He said I had to start working on the farm. But Miss Spencer came to see him and Ma. She told them I was one of her smartest students. She said it would be a shame for me to have to quit school. After she got through talking to them, Pa finally agreed. Of course, it was Ma that really made him change his mind."

"Your mother told me that you used to say you wanted to be a doctor."

Tad lifted his head, his eyes wide. "She did? I haven't said that to anybody in a long time, except Miss Spencer and her father. They told me that if God wanted me to be a doctor, He'd make a way for it to happen."

"They're right. I'll pray for you, Tad."

"Thanks, Mr. Luckett."

The front door opened, and Dr. Spencer trudged inside. His stooped shoulders and tired eyes looked as if they should belong to a man twenty years older. He stopped at Tad's bedside and set his medical bag on the floor. "How are you feeling today?"

"Much better, Dr. Spencer."

"Good. That's what I like to hear." He glanced at Daniel. "You know this young man is going to take over my practice someday. We're already working on it. Aren't we, Tad?"

Tad's pale face lit up, and he grinned. "We are."

Dr. Spencer looked around the room and frowned. "Where's your mother? She hasn't gotten three feet away from you since you got sick."

"I'm right here." Martha bustled from the kitchen and hurried toward them. "We were beginning to get worried about you."

Dr. Spencer rubbed the back of his neck and stretched. "I visited all the homes that have sickness. I was glad to see most of the patients are improving. There's a few that I'm still worried about, but things are beginning to look better. We haven't had any new cases in two weeks."

"Maybe that means it's about over," Daniel said.

"Could be. We'll just have to keep praying. Which reminds me. . ." Dr. Spencer turned to Daniel. "I stopped by to see Reverend Somers. We haven't had any church services since this thing started. Some of the folks have said they'd like to have worship on Sunday, but Reverend Somers says he doesn't know if he can preach or not. He's taken his wife's death really hard."

Martha's eyebrows arched, and she turned to Daniel. "Then why don't you preach for us?"

"Me?" Daniel looked at Martha as if she'd lost her mind. "I'm not a preacher."

Martha shrugged. "You coulda fooled me. The way you been spouting Bible verses and praying by everybody's beds around here, you sure look like a preacher to me."

Dr. Spencer chuckled. "I guess we agree, Martha. That's exactly what I told Reverend Somers. He thought it was a great idea."

Tad pushed up on his elbows. "I sure wish I was well enough so I could be there to hear you, Mr. Luckett."

Daniel held up his hands in protest and took a step back. "I'm telling all of you I'm not a preacher. Maybe somebody else will do it."

Martha shook her head. "No, we want you to preach."

"But I don't feel like I'm qualified. I still have so much to learn about the Bible."

"We never stop learning, Daniel." Dr. Spencer cocked an eyebrow and peered over the top of his spectacles. "You said you've been studying the Bible. Have you ever run across a verse in the Bible where Paul is talking about how he's learned to be content in whatever state he's in?"

Daniel swallowed. "Yes sir."

"What did he say?"

Daniel closed his eyes and recalled the verse that had helped change his life. He quoted, " 'I can do all things through Christ which strengtheneth me.' "

Dr. Spencer chuckled and spread his hands as if declaring victory. "Right. So what do we need to tell Reverend Somers about Sunday?"

The lump in Daniel's throat grew larger. "Tell him I'll be glad to lead the services," he whispered.

Martha clapped her hands and smiled. "Good. Now that

Tad's better, I'll be able to leave him to come hear you. I know we gonna have a great day at church."

Daniel could only nod. When he'd attended Willow Bend Church the summer before, he would never have believed that he would ever stand in the pulpit and tell the people of Willow Bend how much God loved them. Dr. Spencer was right. God's ways were too mysterious for anybody to understand. All Daniel could do was accept them in faith and obey.

He opened his mouth to thank Dr. Spencer, but the sound of running footsteps caused him to whirl and face Tave's room. Savannah stood in the doorway, her face white.

"Dr. Spencer, Daniel, come quickly."

Fear rooted Daniel to the spot, and he didn't know if he could move. Clenching his fists at his sides, he rushed forward past Savannah and hurried to Tave's bedside. If she was dying, he had to tell her one more time how much he loved her.

fifteen

"Wh–what is it, Savannah?" Dr. Spencer's strained voice held the fear Daniel felt in his heart.

"I think she's waking up."

Daniel dropped to his knees and cupped Tave's hand in both of his. He stared into her face. Her eyelids fluttered and then were still. He looked up at Dr. Spencer, who stood beside him. "What's happening? Is she all right?"

Dr. Spencer nudged him to scoot aside. "Let me check her."

Daniel hardly breathed as Dr. Spencer pulled his stethoscope from his bag and listened to Tave's heart. After a moment, he grasped her arm and checked her pulse. A slow smile covered his lips. "Her heart rate is better." He turned to Savannah. "Has there been any hemorrhaging today?"

Savannah shook her head. "Not since yesterday. And she's kept down everything we've fed her today."

He smiled and pushed to his feet. "Good. Maybe we've turned a corner here. We'll keep a close watch until we know for sure."

Daniel exhaled and covered his face with his hands. "I was so scared when I came in here. I thought she might be dying."

Dr. Spencer put his hand on Daniel's shoulder. "If she lives—and now I think she will—we will have to give God the thanks for bringing you back here, Daniel. Even if she hasn't indicated it, I think she knew you were here."

Tears blinded Daniel. "Do you really think so?"

"I do." He took a deep breath and turned to Savannah. "Now, if you think you can spare me awhile, I'm going to lie down in my office. I think I can sleep now."

Savannah put her arms around Dr. Spencer's shoulders and hugged him. "You go on. Daniel and I will keep watch over Tave."

With one last glance at his daughter, Dr. Spencer shuffled from the room, and Daniel sank down in the chair next to the bed. He leaned forward and touched her forehead. It felt cool to his touch, and he smiled.

"I think her fever's down."

Savannah placed her hand on Daniel's shoulder. "I really think we've reached the turning point. She seems to be sleeping peacefully. I'm going in the kitchen to help Mamie with supper. If you need me, call out."

"I will." He reached out and caught Savannah's hand as she turned to leave. "I want to thank you again for taking care of Tave while she's been sick. I know it hasn't been easy for you being away from your children."

"I've been home more than you realize, but I'm blessed to have good friends at Cottonwood who are taking care of Gabby and Vance while I'm gone. I know Tave would have done the same for me."

"Yes, she would have."

Savannah walked from the room, and Daniel leaned over and grasped Tave's hand. "It's time for you to come back to us, Tave. I need you. Open your eyes and look at me."

There was no movement. He took a deep breath and began to talk to her as he had done so often since he'd been back. He related every memory he had of their time together the summer before, from the night he awoke to see her sitting beside his bed to the day he left for Montgomery. He told her how beautiful she'd been in the lavender and white dress the Sunday they went on the picnic, and how funny she looked when she fell playing hopscotch. He leaned closer and whispered how he had lain awake nights and wished he had kissed her that day. It would have been a memory to treasure.

The longer he talked, the more his heart ached. She teetered between life and death, and he wanted her to live so badly. A thought struck him. Maybe God had need of Tave. Even though it would be difficult, that thought could prove comforting if she died.

Something told him, though, that she wasn't going to die. She was going to live, and they were going to have a full life together.

He brought her hand to his lips and kissed her fingers. Still holding it tightly, he leaned closer. "You're going to live, Tave, and as soon as you feel like it, we'll be married. And when we are, I'm going to take you to Selma for a wedding trip. When we get there, I'm going to find a studio and have a daguerreotype made of you to set on our mantel. We'll tell our children that it was made on the happiest day of our lives. Then when we get through at the studio, we're going to do something else you've always wanted. We're going to dinner at the St. James."

He kissed her fingers again. "I know I'll be the envy of every man in the hotel when I escort my beautiful wife into the dining room. So you've got to get well. I've got plans, and you have to help me get ready. How about it? Does all this sound good to you?"

Her lips twitched, and then her fingers pressed against his. His breath caught in his throat. He wasn't sure if he'd imagined it or not. He squeezed her hand, and her fingers responded with gentle pressure. His heart nearly burst with joy. "Good," he whispered. "Now you get some rest, and we'll talk about it when you wake up."

There was no more movement, and after a few minutes, Daniel slipped to his knees. As he had done so often since he'd returned to Willow Bend, he prayed and begged God to spare the woman he loved.

❧

The clock in Dr. Spencer's office chimed midnight, and Daniel stirred in his chair. He hadn't meant to drop off to sleep, but he must have. In a rocker beside him, Savannah slept soundly. She'd dropped off soon after sitting down.

He didn't know how she'd kept going for the past few days. She hardly slept and had devoted every minute to those so ill. Mamie had done the same, as well as Martha and several other ladies from the church.

Working together to care for the sick these past few days had forged a bond between all of them. For the first time in years, Daniel felt like he'd found a place to call home with the people of Willow Bend. Because of the people he'd met here a year ago, he'd also come home to God, and that was the best part. Now if Tave would only recover, life would be perfect.

The bed creaked, and he straightened in his chair. Had she moved? He picked up the oil lamp that they kept burning all night and held it closer to her face. She frowned as if the light caused her pain, and he set it back down.

He knelt beside her bed and stroked her forehead. "Tave, do you need something? Open your eyes, and tell me what you want."

Her mouth twitched, and her eyelids fluttered. He grabbed

her hand and squeezed it.

"You can do it. Open your eyes, and look at me."

She frowned as her eyelids fluttered again, and then her eyes popped open. She stared up and blinked several times. Her tongue licked at her lips, and she turned her head toward the window as if she was staring into the darkness.

He pressed her hand again. "Tave, it's Daniel. Look at me."

The frown on her face deepened, and she turned her head toward him. Even in the soft light, her face, framed by her hair spread out on the pillow, appeared pale and almost lifeless. She blinked several times before recognition flashed in her eyes.

Her mouth spread in a weak smile. "Daniel," she whispered, "is it really you?"

He fought to hold back tears and grasped her hand tighter. "I'm here."

She frowned again. "Wh—where am I?"

"At your father's office. You've been very sick, but you're going to be all right now." He kissed her fingers. "Everything's going to be all right now."

Behind him, Savannah stirred in the rocker, and he touched her arm. "Savannah, wake up."

She jerked upright at his touch. "What's wrong? Is she worse?"

He smiled. "No, she's awake. Stay with her, and I'll get her father."

Savannah dropped to her knees beside the bed, tears running down her cheeks. "Oh Tave, I'm so glad you're back with us. I've missed you so much."

Daniel started to rise, but Tave held on to his hand. "You're not leaving me, are you?"

He put his hand on her head and stroked her hair. "I'm

going to get your father. He made me promise to wake him the minute you opened your eyes." He leaned closer and stared into her eyes. "You don't have to worry about me ever leaving again. I plan on staying with you for the rest of my life."

❧

Four weeks later Tave sat on the porch of her father's office. Upriver she could hear the rumble of the *Liberty Queen*'s whistle announcing its arrival at the Willow Bend docks. With the yellow fever epidemic over, travel had commenced on the Alabama River once again. Tave wondered if there would be any passengers getting off today.

The office door opened, and her father stepped onto the porch. He walked over to one of the posts that supported the roof and leaned against it as he stared toward the river. "I heard the whistle."

Tave nodded. "That should be the *Liberty Queen*. It's about time for her trip downriver."

Her father smiled. "I don't think we're going to see the steamboats for very much longer."

Tave rose and went to stand beside her father. "Why do you say that?"

"Like you're always telling me, for everything there is a season. The railroad is going to replace the steamboats." He straightened and took a deep breath. "But we've got a few years left with them, I think. I'm sure going to miss them when they're gone."

Tave had never given a thought to the fact that the sleek ships she loved might disappear, but she now realized it was possible. She looped her arm through her father's. "I'll miss them, too."

He patted her hand and glanced around. "Where's Daniel? I haven't seen him since early this morning."

Tave laughed and went back to sit in her chair. "He's visiting out at the Ramsey farm. They haven't come to church since they moved here, and he thought he'd give them an invitation."

Dr. Spencer shook his head. "He's quite different from the young man who came to us last summer. I knew God could change his life, but I have to admit I didn't expect such a drastic difference. Can you believe he's preaching?"

Tave smoothed her skirt and chuckled. "I think that was one of my biggest surprises. But he does a wonderful job, and I'm so proud of him I could burst."

"Well, Reverend Somers was happy to have him fill in for him. I think a trip was just what our pastor needed. His wife's death has hit him hard. You know, he'd asked the church to be looking for his replacement this year so he and his wife could move closer to their children. Now I wonder what he'll do."

"I do, too."

Tave looked down to the far end of the street, and her heart thudded at the sight of Daniel riding toward them. He reined the horse to a stop in front of the office, dismounted, and tied the horse to the hitching post. Taking off his hat, he pounded it against his pants' legs. Dust swirled from the clothes.

Grinning, he stepped onto the porch. "The roads are mighty dusty today."

Dr. Spencer cocked an eyebrow. "You don't say. Who would've thought Alabama roads would be dusty in August?"

Daniel shook his head, walked over to Tave, and kissed her on the cheek. "Your father's making fun of me."

She smiled up at him. "Only because he likes you so much."

He smiled. "That's good, because I'm hoping he'll let me marry his daughter."

Dr. Spencer cleared his throat. "I've heard a lot about that wedding, but nobody's told me what the date is. Haven't you two decided yet?"

Tave nodded. "We talked about it last night. If it's all right with you, we'd like to have it the first Sunday afternoon in September."

Dr. Spencer pursed his mouth. "That sounds good to me. After all we've been through in the past few months, I think a wedding celebration is just what we need."

The *Liberty Queen*'s whistle rumbled from the docks, and Tave stared toward the big boat. Daniel turned to look at the impressive steamboat, and Tave rose to stand beside him. She put her hand on his arm. "Do you miss the river, Daniel? Do you want to go back to it?"

His eyes registered surprise. "No. Why would you think that?"

"Well, you're going to have to find work somewhere. I thought maybe you wanted to do that."

He put his arm around her waist and drew her close. "I'm never going to do anything that will take me away from you again. I don't know what the Lord has in mind for me, but He'll provide for us, Tave. I have faith that He'll show me what I'm to do."

She snuggled closer to him. "That's good enough for me."

They stared back at the boat that had now docked and the gangway that had lowered. Passengers began to stream up the hill toward Mr. Perkins's store. Dr. Spencer put his hands in his pockets and studied the people walking up the bluff. "I guess Mr. Perkins can expect an increase in sales today. He always likes to see the boats dock."

Tave's eyes grew wide, and she pointed at a man who appeared at the top of the bluff. "Look, it's Reverend Somers. I didn't know he was coming back today."

"I didn't either," Daniel said.

She started to wave to him, but she felt Daniel stiffen next to her. She glanced up at him. "What is it?" she asked.

He pointed to a man and woman who walked behind Reverend Somers. "That's the couple I told you about in Montgomery, the Collinses. They're the ones I prayed with on the boat."

Reverend Somers spied them, and a big smile covered his face. He turned to the man and woman behind him and pointed to the office porch. All three of them headed that way.

When they stopped on the street in front of the office, Dr. Spencer went down the steps and stuck out his hand to Reverend Somers. "Glad to have you back. We've missed you."

Tave tried to hide her shock at how the preacher had aged since she last saw him. His hair seemed whiter, and his cheeks appeared sunken. He gestured toward the people behind him. "These are my dear friends Lydia and Herbert Collins. You may remember meeting them when Mary was so sick."

Dr. Spencer shook hands with the man. "I do. It's good to have you folks visit Willow Bend again."

Lydia Collins's eyes lit up when Daniel and Tave stepped to the street. She turned to her husband. "Herbert, you may not remember because you were so ill, but this is the young man who prayed with you in Montgomery."

Herbert clamped his hand on Daniel's. "I remember it well. It gave me so much peace. I'm sorry I'm so late in thanking you."

Daniel shook his head. "There's no need for thanks. I was

glad I could help. I'm glad to see you recovered." He turned to Tave. "This is Dr. Spencer's daughter, Tave."

Mrs. Collins smiled. "Ah yes, the young woman you asked if I knew. I see you found her."

Daniel's face turned crimson. "Yes, ma'am, I did."

Dr. Spencer chuckled and patted Daniel on the back before he directed his attention to the Collinses. "How long are you folks planning on staying in Willow Bend?"

Reverend Somers and Mr. Collins glanced at each other, and Mr. Collins cleared his throat. "That depends on a few things. I wonder, Dr. Spencer, if you would allow my wife to visit with your daughter while Thomas and I have a few words inside with Mr. Luckett? Of course, you may join us if you wish."

A puzzled expression crossed Daniel's face, and he glanced at Tave, then her father. "You want to talk to me?"

"Yes. We have some things we'd like to discuss."

Dr. Spencer stepped back on the porch and opened the door. "Feel free to use my office. And Tave will entertain you, Mrs. Collins, but I'm not sure I should join you."

Daniel walked to Dr. Spencer. "I don't know what they want to say to me, but I'd like to have you with me. After all, you're the only father I've ever known."

Tave's heart thudded at the moisture her father blinked from his eyes before he turned and walked through the door.

"Then come on in, Son. Let's see what these men want to talk to you about."

sixteen

Tave fidgeted in her chair and tried to concentrate on what Lydia Collins was saying, but her mind was on the conversation going on behind the closed door to her father's office. She wanted to get up and burst through the front door, but that would embarrass Daniel and her father. Difficult as it was, she was going to have to wait to find out what was being discussed inside.

She directed her attention back to Lydia, who continued speaking as if she hadn't noticed Tave's distraction. "I can't tell you how much we appreciated Daniel coming on board when we were in Montgomery. No one else wanted to come near us. They were afraid of catching yellow fever." She reached over and touched Tave's arm. "And Thomas tells us that you have been ill with it also."

"I have been, but I'm recovering. We lost a lot of friends during the epidemic, but we're thankful that it seems to be over now."

Tave glanced at the door, pushed up from her chair, and took a few steps toward it before she changed directions and went to stand at the edge of the steps. Lydia laughed and came to stand beside her.

"I know you're wondering what's going on, but I'm sure they'll be through soon. Then Daniel will tell you all about it."

Tave nodded and smiled. "Daniel and I are going to be married, you know."

Lydia's eyes lit up. "Thomas told us that. I'm very happy

for you. Maybe you and Daniel will visit Herbert and me in Selma sometime."

"Maybe." Before she could say more, the door opened, and Reverend Somers and Lydia's husband stepped onto the porch. Daniel followed them outside and stuck out his hand. "I still can't believe what's just happened, but I promise I'll pray about it."

Reverend Somers shook Daniel's hand. "Let us know as soon as you reach a decision. Herbert and Lydia will be staying with me for a few days."

"I will."

Lydia took Tave's hand in hers. "It was so good to meet you. I hope we'll see more of each other in the future."

"I hope so, too."

Tave watched as the three guests walked down the steps and headed for the livery stable. She was about to ask Daniel what had happened when her father stepped onto the porch. "I think you two have a lot to talk about. I'll be in my office if you need me."

Daniel took her hand and led her back to the chairs. When they were seated, he faced her. "I can't believe what has just happened."

Tave didn't know whether to be scared or excited. She frowned and squeezed his hand. "If you don't tell me what's going on right now, Daniel Luckett, I'm going to start screaming."

He leaned back in the chair and laughed. "Reverend Somers has wanted to leave Willow Bend Church for a while, but he didn't know who could take over as pastor. He told Reverend Collins how I'd filled in, and Reverend Collins remembered me from our meeting in Montgomery. They want me to take Reverend Somers's place."

Tave's mouth gaped open. "They want you to be the pastor?"

He nodded. "Reverend Somers said that all the people really like me, and he thought they needed somebody young to take over."

"What did you say?"

Daniel shrugged. "Well, I told them I wasn't a real preacher. I'm not ordained. I just study the Bible, and I still have a lot to learn."

Tave scooted to the edge of her chair. "And?"

"And they said that didn't matter. They still learned something new from the Bible every day. I told them we were getting married in a few weeks, and they thought that would be perfect. Reverend Collins said if we'd come to Selma, he would plan an ordination service for me at his church. Then I could come back and start the work here. Reverend Somers said his house belongs to the church, and we can live there. He doesn't want to take all his furniture, and he'll leave some of it for us."

Tave stood up and pressed her hand to her forehead. "I can't believe this." She paced across the porch, turned, and retraced her steps. "A preacher? I never expected this." She stopped in front of him. "Did you give them an answer?"

He rose and took her hand. "I told them I'd pray about it, but I wanted to talk to you first and see what you thought."

His blue eyes stared at her, and she recalled the day he'd been shot and had looked up at her. She'd stared into the depths of his eyes and had somehow known God had great plans for him. She'd prayed for him, and God had proven her right by bringing them to this moment.

She cupped his face with her other hand. "I think you'll make a wonderful preacher."

He bit his lip. "But what about you? It won't be easy being the wife of a pastor."

She smiled. "I know, but if that's what God has planned for us, we'll make it fine."

He pulled her to him and hugged her then held her at arm's length and smiled. "I wish I knew where that gambler that shot me is right now. I'd sure like to shake his hand and thank him for doing me a favor. The day he shot me was the luckiest day of my life."

❧

Daniel ran his finger around the inside rim of his shirt collar and then tugged at the tie knotted at his neck. He didn't know if it really was the hottest day of the year, or if he was perspiring because he was so nervous. Across the room, Dante Rinaldi leaned back in a chair and scraped underneath his fingernails with the tip of a pocketknife. He didn't appear hot at all.

Dante glanced up and grinned. "It won't be long now. The bride and her father should be arriving outside the church any minute."

Daniel rubbed the back of his neck and took a deep breath. "Is it hot in here to you?"

Dante laughed and stood up. "It's just nerves. I doubt if there ever was a man who wasn't nervous on his wedding day."

Daniel ran his hands down the front of the new suit he'd bought at Mr. Perkins's store. "Do I look all right?"

Dante slapped him on the back. "You look fine, but don't worry. Nobody's going to be looking at you. Everybody's eyes are going to be on Tave."

The thought made him smile, and he felt his face grow warm. "Yeah, I guess you're right. I think I am a little scared.

A lot's happened to me in the past few weeks. I'm about to become the pastor of a church, and the most wonderful woman in the world is marrying me."

Dante nodded. "You remind me of how I felt when Savannah and I got married. I was scared to death that day. We didn't have any family, and I had to drive her to the church. All the way to her house, I was scared she'd changed her mind."

"But she didn't."

Dante's eyes grew wistful. "No, she didn't. And I thought I had to be the luckiest man in the world. Just like you feel today."

They both grew silent, and Daniel knew Dante had to be thinking of his wife just as Daniel was now thanking God for Tave. "Dante, I appreciate your standing up with me today. You're a good friend."

Dante smiled. "And so are you, Daniel. Of course from now on, I guess I'm going to have to be on my best behavior around you."

"Why?"

"Because you're going to be my pastor. I don't want to come to church and hear you preaching to me about all the bad things you see me doing."

A vision of standing in the pulpit and lashing out at the congregation over their sins flashed into Daniel's mind, and he laughed out loud. "Don't worry. I'm sure God just wants me to preach His Word."

"Sounds like you're going to make it fine, my friend."

The door opened, and Reverend Somers stepped into the room. "Well, Tave and her father are at the front door of the church. Are you ready to go meet your bride, Daniel?"

The heat he'd felt a few minutes earlier disappeared, and his spirit calmed. What he'd dreamed about and thought impossible was about to happen. Tave was going to be his wife. He breathed one more prayer of thanks and took a deep breath.

"I'm ready."

❧

Her father crooked his arm and smiled down at Tave. She slipped her arm through his and gazed up at the dear man who had dedicated his life to caring for her. Soon she would be Daniel's wife, and perhaps someday she would be someone's mother. But in her heart, she would always be her father's little girl.

Tears flooded her eyes. "Oh, Poppa, I'm scared."

He smiled and patted her hand. "You shouldn't be. You're about to start a wonderful new life with a man who loves you very much, and you're going to be the wife of a preacher. How could I want any more for you?"

"But what about you? Who will take care of you?"

He chuckled. "Don't worry about me. I can take care of myself. Besides, it's not like you're moving off to the far side of the earth. You're going to be right outside of town. And you'll come to my office and help out some."

"I will." She tilted her head and stared up at him. "Do you think I did the right thing giving up my job at the school?"

"I think so. Daniel's going to need a wife to help him, and I know God's going to use you in a great way."

The church door opened, and Tad Thompson grinned at them from inside. "Miss Bonnie's about to start playing the pump organ, Miss Spencer. Are you ready?"

She nodded. "I am." She stood on tiptoes and kissed her father on the cheek. "I love you, Poppa."

He stared into her face, and a tear glistened in the corner of his eye. "I love you, too, darling. You look just like your mother today. I just wish she could be here to see you."

The first chords wheezed from the organ, and Tave and her father stepped to the door. At the end of the aisle, Daniel stood waiting for her.

❧

Nothing could have prepared Daniel for the vision Tave presented as she walked down the aisle on the arm of her father. She wore her mother's wedding dress, and to him, she looked like a queen, just as Dr. Spencer had thought of his bride many years before.

Her gaze locked with his, and the assembled friends vanished from Daniel's vision. In the stillness of the church, he saw only her. His soul reached out to her in that moment, and he felt a bonding like he'd never known in his life. This was the woman God had chosen for him, and he would cherish her for the rest of his life.

Daniel's breath caught in his throat as they stopped beside him. He smiled at her before he directed his attention to Reverend Somers.

The pastor stepped forward and looked from Tave to her father. "Who gives this woman in marriage?"

"I do," Dr. Spencer replied. He leaned over, kissed Tave on the cheek, and placed her hand in Daniel's. With a smile on his face, he turned and walked to his seat on the front pew.

Tave's hand felt warm in his, and Daniel's pulse pounded. He wrapped his fingers around hers and directed his attention back to the pastor.

"Dearly beloved," Reverend Somers said.

Daniel heard the drone of the pastor's voice, but he could only concentrate on Tave next to him. He had little recollection of the responses he made to the questions asked, but from the shy smile Tave directed at him, he knew he answered.

Then with the final vow taken, Reverend Somers uttered

the words that sent Daniel's heart soaring. "I now pronounce you man and wife."

Daniel and Tave turned to face the congregation, and she slipped her arm through his. They walked up the aisle, nodding to those on each side, and made their way to the door. Outside, Dante and Savannah waited in their buggy to drive them back to her father's house. There they would receive all their friends who'd come to share this day with them.

Daniel helped Tave into the backseat and climbed in beside her. Savannah reached back and squeezed Tave's hand. "It was a beautiful wedding. You look so happy."

Tave's eyes sparkled, and she gazed up at Daniel. "I've never been happier."

Daniel stared into his wife's eyes and marveled at how God had blessed him. He had left home after his mother's death and wandered for years. In all that time, he'd been consumed with hatred that threatened to destroy him. Tave and her father had shown him how to find peace through faith in God, and he had been blessed more than he would ever have thought possible.

He leaned over and whispered in his wife's ear. "I can still hardly believe it. We're married."

She grinned. "Yes we are, Mr. Luckett."

He pulled her close. "I love you, Mrs. Luckett."

Mrs. Luckett. No words had ever sounded sweeter to him.

❧

Tave stood on the balcony outside their room at the St. James Hotel and stared at the river that wound past. Two boys, their fishhooks in the water, sat on the bank not far upstream. They hadn't moved since she'd been watching them.

The door behind her opened, and she sensed Daniel's presence. He walked up behind her, circled her waist with his arms, and drew her back to rest against his chest. He bent forward and whispered in her ear. "What are you doing out here?"

His breath tickled her ear, and she smiled. "I'm looking at the river. I think it's so beautiful when the sun's going down, and the last rays are reflecting off the surface."

He tightened his arms around her. "That's not the only beautiful thing I see out here."

She laughed and patted his hands. "I'll assume you're talking about me, so I'll take that as a compliment."

"You should." He rested his cheek against her, and they stared across the water.

She laid her head back against his chest. "I thought the ordination service was beautiful today. I was so proud of you. I shed a few tears when you addressed the group afterward. I know you're going to be a great pastor."

"We won't have a lot of money, but we'll be happy because God will take care of us. We'll always have what we need. I have faith that God will provide for us."

"I do, too." A thought flashed across her mind, and she laughed. "I just remembered something."

"What?"

"The day I first saw you, Savannah had driven me from the school to Poppa's office. We were talking about falling in love. I told her that sometimes my romantic side wished that I could meet a handsome young man who would sweep me off my feet, but I doubted that would ever happen. Less than five minutes later, I saw you for the first time."

He nuzzled her ear. "And what did you think?"

She laughed. "I gave you up for dead. But then you opened your eyes. When I stared into those blue eyes, it was as if God told me I had to save you. It was as if I knew God had great plans for you."

"For us, Tave." He kissed her hair. "We had a visitor while you were out here enjoying the scenery."

She turned in his arms to stare up at him. "Who?"

He released her, reached in his pocket, and drew out an embossed leather case. Her eyes grew wide with excitement. "My daguerreotype came."

He nodded and opened it. "What do you think?"

She took the picture in her hand and stared at the shiny portrait they'd had made the day before. She was seated in a chair, her wedding dress spread out and her hands clasped in her lap. Her chin trembled, and she fought to hold back the tears. "I look just like my mother."

"Since your father gave you the one of your mother, I think we need to put the two of them side by side on the mantel in our new home. What do you think?"

She threw her arms around his neck and drew him close. "Thank you, Daniel, for having this made for me. I love you so much."

"And I love you."

Downriver, a steamboat whistle sounded, and Daniel glanced at the river. "That sounds like the *Carrie Davis* coming upriver."

"I wonder if some of the passengers will stay here tonight."

"We'll soon know." He pulled out his pocket watch. "It's almost time to eat. Are you hungry?"

She closed the daguerreotype case and pressed her hands to her stomach. "I'm starved, Mr. Luckett."

He smiled, and her heart leaped at the love she saw in his eyes. "Good. There's a table waiting for us in the dining room." He crooked his arm and extended it to her. "Mrs. Luckett, it would be my honor to escort you to dinner at the St. James."

A Letter To Our Readers

Dear Reader:
In order that we might better contribute to your reading enjoyment, we would appreciate your taking a few minutes to respond to the following questions. We welcome your comments and read each form and letter we receive. When completed, please return to the following:

Fiction Editor
Heartsong Presents
PO Box 719
Uhrichsville, Ohio 44683

1. Did you enjoy reading *Dinner at the St. James* by Sandra Robbins?
   ❑ Very much! I would like to see more books by this author!
   ❑ Moderately. I would have enjoyed it more if

   _____

   _____

   _____

2. Are you a member of **Heartsong Presents**? ❑ Yes ❑ No
   If no, where did you purchase this book? _____

   _____

3. How would you rate, on a scale from 1 (poor) to 5 (superior), the cover design? _____

4. On a scale from 1 (poor) to 10 (superior), please rate the following elements.

   ____ Heroine   ____ Plot
   ____ Hero   ____ Inspirational theme
   ____ Setting   ____ Secondary characters

5. These characters were special because? _____
_____
_____

6. How has this book inspired your life? _____
_____
_____

7. What settings would you like to see covered in future
   Heartsong Presents books? _____
_____
_____

8. What are some inspirational themes you would like to see
   treated in future books? _____
_____
_____

9. Would you be interested in reading other **Heartsong
   Presents** titles? ❏ Yes ❏ No

10. Please check your age range:
     ❏ Under 18   ❏ 18-24
     ❏ 25-34   ❏ 35-45
     ❏ 46-55   ❏ Over 55

Name _____
Occupation _____
Address _____
City, State, Zip _____
E-mail _____

Presents

Great Inspirational Romance at a Great Price!

Heartsong Presents books are inspirational romances in contemporary and historical settings, designed to give you an enjoyable, spirit-lifting reading experience. You can choose wonderfully written titles from some of today's best authors like Wanda E. Brunstetter, Mary Connealy, Susan Page Davis, Cathy Marie Hake, Joyce Livingston, and many others.

When ordering quantities less than six, above titles are $3.99 each.
Not all titles may be available at time of order.

HEARTSONG PRESENTS

If you love Christian romance...

$12.⁹⁹

You'll love Heartsong Presents' inspiring and faith-filled romances by today's very best Christian authors...Wanda E. Brunstetter, Mary Connealy, Susan Page Davis, Cathy Marie Hake, and Joyce Livingston, to mention a few!

When you join Heartsong Presents, you'll enjoy four brand-new, mass-market, 176-page books—two contemporary and two historical—that will build you up in your faith when you discover God's role in every relationship you read about!

Mass Market 176 Pages

Imagine...four new romances every four weeks—with men and women like you who long to meet the one God has chosen as the love of their lives...all for the low price of $12.99 postpaid.

To join, simply visit www.heartsong presents.com or complete the coupon below and mail it to the address provided.

YES! Sign me up for Heartsong!